D1046321

ARE YOU ON OUR EMAIL LIST?

Sign up on our website

WWW.THECARTELPUBLICATIONS.COM

OR TEXT THE WORD: CARTELBOOKS
TO 22828
FOR PRIZES, CONTESTS, ETC.

CARTEL PUBLICATIONS
PRESENTS

A NOVEL BY

REIGN

FIRST
COMES
Love
THEN COMES
MURDER

PUBLISHER'S NOTE:
This book is a work of fiction. Names, characters, businesses, Organizations, places, events and incidents are the product of the Author's imagination or are used fictionally. Any resemblance of Actual persons, living or dead, events, or locales are entirely co-incidental.

Library of Congress Control Number: 2013941368
ISBN 10: 0989084515

ISBN 13: 9780989084512

Cover Design: Davida Baldwin www.oddballdsgn.com
Editor: Advanced Editorial Services
Graphics: Davida Baldwin
www.thecartelpublications.com
First Edition

Printed in the United States of America

CHECK OUT OTHER TITLES BY
THE CARTEL PUBLICATIONS

What's Poppin' Fam,

I hope all is well in your world! The Cartel Publications continues to move on with the strength of a hurricane, and we love you for keeping us grinding! In addition to our thriving publishing house, T. Styles has partnered with our graphic designer, Vida Baldwin and created, "Mean Girls Magazine". This magazine is geared toward empowering women using real topics and hardcore stories. Make sure you check it out and sign up for their email list via their website,**www.meangirlsmagazine.com**.

Now without further pleasantries, let me jump directly into the novel at hand, "First Comes Love, Then Comes Murder." If you are not prepared to read a phenomenal novel that will not only pull you in, but also make you stroll down memory lane, then you need to get prepared quickly. Reign (T. Styles) has done her homework in this latest contribution to literary history. This novel is incredible and I thoroughly enjoyed it from beginning to end. I know you will too.

Keeping in line with tradition, we want to give respect to a trailblazer paving the way. With that said we would like to recognize:

Skyy is the author of, "Choices"; "Consequences"; "Crossroads" and the last novel in that series, "Full Circle." When I first read these novels I was elated to be able to read a book that resembles my life. Skyy's work is not just lesbian fiction, but it portrays life, love, and heartache that everyone can understand. Make sure you check these titles out if you want to read a great series.

Ok, go 'head and dive in! I'll holla at you in the next novel.

Be Easy!

Charisse "C. Wash" Washington
Vice President
The Cartel Publications
www.thecartelpublications.com
www.twitter.com/cartelbooks
www.facebook.com/cartelpublications

ACKNOWLEDGEMENTS

I acknowledge all Cartel Publications fans. It's amazing how much support you all have given me over the years. I am amazed and blessed to have you in my corner, because I don't know where I would be without you in my life.

This is a hard story about love lost. I hope you enjoy it.

Love,
Reign (T. Styles)

DEDICATION

I dedicate this to my Cartel Publications fans. I love you.

CHAPTER 1

In The Courtroom:

Warm urine streamed down Juliette "Jewels" Madison's inner thighs, as she faced the jam-packed courtroom. To say she was in fear for her life was an understatement. As she released her bladder, she looked down at the puddle forming just below her feet. She observed the judge, and hoped from his higher view, that he couldn't see her mess. This ratchet behavior was unlike Jewels, but unfortunately she had zero control over her bodily functions at the moment, because her nerves were at an all time high. This was serious, for the rest of her young life was on the line.

As her brown eyes observed the crowd, who looked upon her as if they knew her fucking business, she felt disdain in her heart. Who were they to make judgments when they had dirty secrets of their own?

No her marriage wasn't perfect, but then again whose marriage was? She dreaded this day, because she would be forced to tell the world why the man who took her virginity, exposed her to the luxury life, and stole her heart, was now six feet deep.

Jewels' dark brown skin, and her soft black hair, courtesy of her Black and Honduran heritage, was slicked back into a long flowing ponytail. The style was a long way away from the luscious curls that dawned her hair on a regular basis, after she frequented DC's most prestigious hair salons. No, today she resembled an innocent high school student; accept she was on trial for murder.

Although Jewels looked lowly, her female high profile defense team didn't. Whenever attorneys Adele Abigail and Carly Rosalyn accepted a new client, it was widely known that their defendant would be deemed not guilty. So the question was never guilt or innocent when it came to their clients, but how would the inventive duo work their magic.

After Judge Geoff Morrison addressed the courtroom, the prosecutor, Howard Murray, approached Juliette who was on the stand trying to reduce her shivers. This was a career case for him and he knew it. If he were able to convince the world that the seemingly innocent Juliette Madison, was nothing more than a heartless and greedy, murderer, he would set the stage for a long prosperous career.

"Please state your first and last name for the court," Howard said, barely able to breathe due to the three hundred and fifty pounds that occupied his 5'7 inch frame.

"My name is Juliette Madison," she said lightly, looking down at her trembling fingers, before stuffing them in between her damp, pissy thighs.

"Please spell your last name for the record."

"R...A...M...O...S."

It wasn't until the courtroom gasped that she realized her error. She looked at her attorneys, and the judge, wondering how to repair the major mistake. But before she could right her wrong, the prosecution used the opportunity to highlight her blunder.

He approached the stand. "I'm sorry, but I thought you said your name was Juliette Madison," he said slyly, believing he was on to something big. "So are you Juliette Madison or not?"

"Uh...I...my name is Juliette Madison," she stuttered, "and my last name is spelled M...A...D...I...S...O...N."

With a smirk he asked, "Well who is Ramos?"

"I don't know," she lied. "I was nervous, and I...I mean...the name just came from somewhere."

"Mrs. Madison, were you or were you not born in the United States of America?"

"I object," Adele yelled. "The prosecution is implying that there aren't any American citizens with the last name Ramos. His question is racist at best."

"Sustained". Judge Morrison ruled.

"I'll rephrase the question, your honor. "Where were you born?"

"I am a US citizen," Juliette lied. "And I was born in this country."

● ● ●

San Pedro Sula, Honduras
June 5, 1992

The Truth:

Ten year old Juliette, who was born Alejandra Ramos, sat next to her friend on a beaten down brown cloth couch, in a man's house she didn't know. Just an hour earlier she was playing in the back yard with the only doll she owned, and the next minute she was sitting with Ana Christina, both girls faces were covered in heavy makeup.

When Juliette was taken, her uncle, a career drug addict, received some money from a stranger in a white pick up truck, before both of them were stuffed inside the back of the vehicle against their will. Why had her uncle Javier brought them there? She was left in his care when her mother Kathia Ramos went to work earlier, to care for the children of a wealthy family. Juliette was so confused, and she wanted her mother.

Although Ana was doing her best to strike up conversation, to keep her mind off of the fear, Juliette could not help but focus on the door, where the Truck Man went into a room with another little girl and closed the door behind him. Although faint, she could hear the child telling him to stop, and that he was hurting her. The girl's cries were almost muted due to his heavy panting.

When the door opened, and the little girl was pushed out of the room, her pink dress covered in blood, the monster, an American, waved Ana over, in an effort to steal her innocence too.

Ana stood up, and Juliette observed her closely as she walked toward the bedroom. Although she wasn't sure why, she had a feeling that when Ana returned she wouldn't be the same, and she wanted to remember her friend just the way that she was.

When the door closed to the bedroom, the wooden front door to the house came crashing down. In rushed all three hundred pounds of Kathia Ramos, her face screwed up in anger, because her only child was taken yet again, and possibly violated like so many others in their country.

When she spotted her daughter on the filthy sofa, without a word, she gripped her hand with a force so strong, the socket of Juliette's arm popped out of place. Kathia paid no attention to her daughter's painful cries;

she just continued to haul her child away from the scene with a loose arm. When they were a safe distance away, she pushed Juliette's arm back in place, as the sound of gunfire went off in the background. But the noise was as normal to the natives who lived in Honduras, as air planes flying over the blue skies in America. San Pedro Sula was the murder capital of the world, where no less than three people were *intentionally* murdered everyday.

After what seemed like an eternity walking, Juliette and Kathia arrived at a small brick building. Spread out on the front was a large red sign that read SWEET RICE CHARITY. Mitch McKenzie, a successful drug dealer, established the foundation in an effort to aid the people of the country who were in need. And, Kathia couldn't be more grateful for the building's presence, because she knew she could not go home, until she killed her brother.

Kathia rushed through the halls of the charity, with Juliette's hand still in hers. When she reached a cream door, she knocked on it heavily, like she was the police. When a woman who resembled Kathia appeared from the other side, Juliette wondered if she was related to her.

Maricel Rivas, a citizen of America, welcomed them both into the cramped office. Although she was of no relation, Maricel treated Kathia like she was family. Maricel was actually born in Honduras and raised in the United States, but when the opportunity presented itself to work with Sweet Rice Charities, she jumped at it. Armed with an education, when the time was right, Maricel went back to her country, to assist her community. She stayed in Honduras for four months out of the year, and had one month left on her assignment. But since the violence had reached an all time high, she was being shipped back home for her safety. Everyone else in the charity was already gone, but she was the last to leave, and the van picking her up, to take her to the airport was arriving in less than five minutes.

They were speaking in their native language. (English Translation) "Have a seat, Alejandra," Kathia said to her daughter.

Never disobeying her mother, Juliette quickly sat in a chair, across from the tiny desk. When she looked to the left, she saw two huge blue suitcases, next to the entrance of the door.

"Maricel, my brother did it again, he tried to sell my daughter for sex, to an American, to support his drug habit. Had I not come home early, because my spirit said something was off, I'm afraid to think about what would have happened to my dear sweet Alejandra. I know you are leaving today, because of the war with the Cartels, but you must take her with you to America, so that she can have a better life there." She placed her hand over her chest. "My fear is that although I can take care of myself, I can't provide the same security for my daughter, and she may be stolen, raped and murdered while I'm at work, trying to support us."

Just hearing her mother caused Juliette to shiver.

"Kathia, I would love to help you," she said pushing her brown glasses toward her face. "But you know it's not that easy. You have to understand that there are procedures to taking a child to America, and the way you're asking is not one of them. It's not legal."

"Not legal?" She frowned. "But the company you work with has access to a plane, Maricel," she pleaded. "And I know the owner transports drugs in and out of this country. You can take her with you, please."

"I wish I could help you, Kathia," she walked toward her desk, and placed a manila folder into her black leather briefcase. "I truly do, but there is nothing I can do for you, I really am sorry."

"You mean you won't help me, because you don't want to. I know you can do something. I know all about the drugs being transported in and out of my country on those Sweet Rice Charity planes. They don't even go through the same channels as commercial flights."

"I'm sorry, Kathia, I really am, but it's out of my hands."

Kathia stood back and observed the woman, and tried so hard not to hate her. After all, Maricel had done everything she could for Kathia and her family. When they needed food she bought it. When they needed clothing, Maricel provided it. She even arranged to hide Kathia and Juliette when a drug war wreaked havoc on their neighborhood, and bullets rang into the small homes like rain. But this small favor she simply could not do.

"I wish you didn't say that," Kathia said softly, walking up to her. "I truly do."

When Kathia was upon her, without notice, she took her beefy hands and wrapped them around Maricel's neck. Maricel did all she could to fight back but her blows were useless. Nothing was stronger than a mother who wanted so desperately to protect her only child. Maricel never had a chance.

Although it would do her no good, Maricel slapped at Kathia's arms until she didn't have the strength to even keep her eyes open. As she was dying, Kathia watched her eyes roll up into the top of her head. When all she saw was the whites of her eyeballs, she released her corpse, allowing her to thump to the floor.

Remembering that her daughter was present, she looked behind her and was immediately consumed with guilt. Juliette was still sitting in a chair, and a puddle of urine rested under her body. Without another word, and with no time to explain, Kathia yanked her off of the chair, injuring her sore arm again.

"Help me take the things out of this suitcase," Kathia demanded. "We must hurry! The bus is coming shortly!"

Together they opened the largest suitcase, and threw everything inside of it on the floor. When it was empty Kathia got on her knees and addressed her daughter in Spanish.

(English translation) "Alejandra, I know you're frightened, but I can no longer take the risk of something happening to you. So you must get into this suitcase, where you will remain until we reach America."

Her eyes widened and she tried to back up, but her mother, never knowing her strength, yanked her closer. "Mama, I'm scared." She said rubbing her sore arm. "I don't want to go in there. What if I die? What if I can't breathe?"

"Baby," Kathia said as tears flowed down her face, "you will get into that suitcase either willingly or by force. Now I don't want to hurt you. It is the reason I want you away from our country, but I will if I have to so help me God. Now please, Alejandra, get inside of the suitcase and do not delay."

Slowly she did as her mother demanded, until she was zipped into the cloth case. With her daughter taken care of, Kathia found the identification documents belonging to Maricel. To appear more like her, she combed her hair back into a ponytail, snatched the glasses off of Maricel's face, and the name badge off of her chest, to assume her identity. When she was done, she stuffed Maricel's body under the desk, partially out of view.

Ready to play the part, she grabbed some of the clothes on the floor, including a Sweet Rice Charity shirt, and put them on. When she was done she rolled her daughter, who was packed inside of the suitcase outside. The Sweet Rice Charity van was already out front, and the bus driver was packing boxes underneath the bus, and she was immediately concerned.

Kathia, worried that the weight of the packages would weigh down her daughter, attempted to pull the luggage up the steps and onto the bus, until she was stopped.

He also spoke in Spanish. "Ma'am," the driver said touching her on the shoulder from behind, "you have to put your luggage under the bus."

"No, I can't," Kathia advised. "I...I gotta take it with me inside."

"Why?" he observed the suitcase. "What's so special about it?"

"Sir, everything I own is inside of this suitcase."

"Ma'am—"

"Please," she begged. "It's been a long day, and I just lost someone I love about an hour ago. All I want is to protect his precious items, and they are all in this suitcase." She looked at the window. "It won't take up too much space, there isn't hardly anybody on the bus anyway."

The bus driver observed the woman closely and was highly suspicious. "Ma'am, let me see your identification please."

"What?" She placed the suitcase softly down and looked into his eyes. "But why?"

"Because I asked," he held out his hand. "Now give me your identification. I will not repeat myself."

Slowly she dug into Maricel's purse that was dangling on her arm, and retrieved the passport and identification card. With a shaky hand, she handed both of the documents to him. The bus driver remembered seeing Maricel six months earlier, although he didn't know her personally. But with the faint memory he held of Maricel in his mind, he took in the woman before him. In his opinion they looked alike, but if he could remember right, there was a slight difference in their mannerisms, although not enough to detect. Was she the same person or not?

When he remembered they paid him to drive the bus, and not investigate crimes, he handed them back to her.

"I can't let you take this luggage on the bus, but I will put it over the other's until you make it to the airport. Don't worry, your things will be safe with me, I'm an excellent driver."

Relieved he didn't kick her off, and understanding that this was as good as it was going to get she said, "Thank you, that'll have to do."

Kathia was sitting in the front of the Sweet Rice Charity airplane exhausted, and eager to get off. She had achieved the ultimate, and all she wanted to do was hug her daughter, who was under the plane with the rest of the packages. She prayed heavily for hours, that her only child was safe. She still couldn't believe it. She managed to take Maricel's identity, and board the Sweet Rice Charity's plane without being detected.

Although she had never been out of her country, or on a plane for that matter, she was certain that security was not as strict as she thought it should be. The officials were paid to turn a blind eye to what the organization was doing, and she even witnessed a white powder substance leaking from one of the bags under the plane. She hoped her daughter would not catch a drug contact. Kathia had been in Honduras all of her life, and she knew what was going on. The charity was nothing more than a front to transport drugs in and out of the country.

Five hours later, Kathia arrived in Washington DC. She was impatient with the exiting process and felt the people inside weren't moving fast enough. When the doors to the plane finally opened, she pushed her way to the front, knocking over an elderly woman in the process.

Because of the drugs that the charity was transporting, the luggage was not sent through baggage claim. She was given a ticket and told to wait outside while the luggage was being unloaded. When her number was called, corresponding to her bag, she watched as they yanked her suitcase out and threw it to the ground. Her heart dropped quickly as she imagined the type of pain her daughter was in.

She rushed up to it, and snatched it away from the carrier, after giving him her ticket. When she had the bag in her possession, it took everything in her power not to call her daughter's name, praying that she responded. But she needed to be out of everyone's view first, because it would do her no good to come this far, and mess it all up by being premature.

It wasn't until she was away from prying eyes, that she pulled on the side of a building and unzipped the bag. Her daughter's limp body fell out, and her eyes were closed. Wet vomit was all over Juliette's clothing.

"Oh my, God, no," she screamed, scrapping her knees, making them bloody, as she dropped to the ground. "Please, don't be dead, Alejandra! Please, my dear sweet baby!"

When she finally opened her eyes, in a light voice she said, "Mama, I'm okay." She coughed a few times.

Kathia wept over her body, and held her tightly in her arms. After everything she'd gone through, to give her daughter a better life, it worked. It really worked!

"Baby, I'm so sorry for what I had to do, and I pray you forgive me," she said wiping her hair back. "You will never have to be afraid again. Ever," she rocked her in her arms. "I love you, Alejandra. I love you!"

● ● ●

Six Months Later
USA

Juliette sat against a huge office building in downtown DC with her mother. Both of them were hungry, and barefoot. Although they ate out of trashcans, and didn't have a home due to Kathia refusing all help, life was still better than it had been in Honduras. But there was something changing in Kathia. She felt worthless because she had activated a plan to save Juliette, brought her all the way to America, only for them to be living on the streets.

"Oh my goodness! What a beautiful little girl," a middle age black woman said, as she stooped over Juliette and Kathia.

Juliette said, "Gracias," recognizing the word beautiful.

The moment Juliette opened her mouth to thank the woman; Kathia smacked her so hard in the face that her head banged against the brick wall behind her.

In Spanish she scolded her daughter. (English Translation) "What did I tell you? Didn't I say to never use your voice in America, until I say it was okay? You have to be careful, Alejandra. We are in this country illegally, and you never know American motives. Now repeat to me, what did I tell you?"

"To always be perfecting my survival instincts," she said, as tears rolled down her face. Her mother never intentionally hurt her until now, and she didn't know how to cope.

"Ma'am, why did you hit her?" The woman asked, angry at the abuse she just witnessed, due to her compliment. She didn't understand Spanish, so she couldn't understand what Kathia was saying to her daughter.

And Kathia, not understanding English, gave the woman an evil glare hoping she would be afraid and leave them alone.

But when Juliette moaned in pain, Kathia whipped her head in her daughter's direction to see what was wrong.

"Mommy, my head is cut," Juliette said touching the back of her head, and showing her bloody fingers.

"Oh, my Alejandra, I'm so sorry."

When she moved to touch her, Juliette jumped in fear. It was then that Kathia realized that her only child was horrified of her. After everything she did to protect her, she only succeeded in tearing their bond apart. But suddenly Kathia saw things clearly, and knew what she had to do.

She brushed her daughter's hair backward, and looked into her eyes. Kathia knew that her very existence in America was holding Juliette back. So she smiled, kissed her on the forehead and looked out at the road ahead of her.

"Don't remember what is about to happen, remember that I did it because I love you and wanted the best for you. Be careful whom you give your heart to, and always protect yourself, Alejandra. I love you."

Kathia stood up, and as if she were a zombie, stepped off of the curb and into the middle of the street. A Metro bus unable to stop in time, smacked against her huge body, forcing her into a black Cadillac Escalade. Her flesh opened like a dropped watermelon and sprayed into her daughter's face.

Kathia Ramos died instantly.

CHAPTER 2

In The Courtroom:

Outside of two people, Jewels never told anyone else that she was not from America. As far as her attorneys and the prosecution knew, she was a US citizen. Jewels knew she had to be careful about what she revealed, and what she didn't or else it could be used against her.

As the case got underway, everyone in the courtroom was glued to every word she muttered. She was both beautiful and pitiful to watch at the same time, and the world was intrigued.

"Mrs. Madison, where exactly did you meet Marcel?" the prosecutor questioned.

"At work," she said rubbing her hands together, which remained in her lap.

"Oh work...Where did you work, because nothing you told us about your past, seems to add up?"

"I object," Adele yelled. "The prosecution is badgering the witness."

"I'll rephrase the question." he replied. "Juliette, exactly where did you work?"

"In a food truck," she replied. "It was a small job but it paid some of my bills."

"What kind of food truck," he smirked.

"Probably an illegal one." The courtroom laughed a little but then quickly settled down. "They didn't really wash their hands, they overcharged customers for expired food and they didn't have a license." She shrugged.

"Sometimes they paid us under the table and other times they didn't pay us at all."

"If all of these things are true, then why did you work there? I mean, I would never work for an unsavory company."

"Because I needed the job."

"How long were you employed for this food truck, before you met Marcel?"

Even though he was dead, his name still did something to her body. He was her husband, and even in his death, he held a place that nobody else owned. The nigga had her heart, mind and body, and he fucked it all up with his shiftlessness. If anybody should be on trial it should be his bum ass, to hear her tell it. Her marriage wasn't a game as far as she was concerned, but still she ended up getting played.

"I was there for only a few months. I handled the hot dogs, and he handled the tacos," she lied.

"How was it working with him?"

"We worked good together, and it was love at first sight," she smiled. "I still remember that day like it was yesterday."

The Truth:
Winter, 1999

Seventeen year old Juliette was driving down the street with her favorite song *Scrubs* playing on the radio, during a warm winter day. She couldn't believe that the gray steering wheel clutched tightly in her hand, actually belonged to her. Although it was a used Honda Civic, considering the life she led after her mother died, it was a come up.

After that tragic incident, which kept Juliette up late at night, she was placed in a foster home. And because she wouldn't speak, for fear that she'd be taken back to Honduras, most people assumed she was mute and dumb. But, Juliette was far from ignorant. Before long, by listening and observing instead of speaking, Juliette was able to teach herself both written and spoken English. When everyone was asleep, she would practice the English dialect out loud, until she was so good you could no longer detect her Honduran tongue. Still, she refused to speak or write. She also taught herself how to drive at night, by using the cars that belonged to the family members wherever she stayed.

Juliette was moved from foster home to foster home, due to running away. But she had to bounce to save her virginity. Her intoxicating beauty was often too much for lesser men to handle. And when they attempted to rape her, she would fight them off only to be placed into another home.

Her final run came about six months ago. Juliette was living with a newlywed couple, David and Wanda Deville. Because they were young, in their late twenties, they knew how to relate to her, and Juliette had a lot of fun, despite her silence. They were aware that she couldn't speak or write, and they didn't look down upon her. They would take her to the movies, fancy restaurants, and even bought her designer clothing for school. Things were looking up for Juliette, and she was thankful for her new family.

Finally, six months before Christmas, she was thinking about letting them in on her secret. She didn't have money, but she hoped the gift of honesty about her past would suffice. Besides, she had grown to love them both, and wanted to thank them for loving her back, and their hospitality.

But the moment she came home from school, on the day she made up her mind to talk, Wanda slapped her violently in the face. At first Juliette didn't know who struck her. But when her eyes focused, she saw it was Wanda. She was crying hysterically over Juliette, while clutching a pair of Juliette's soiled underwear in her hand.

"You fucking sleeping with my husband, bitch?" she sobbed. "After everything I did for you, this is how you repay me?" She dragged her into the house, and slammed the door.

Juliette tossed her book bag down and tried to crawl away. But Wanda grabbed her by her hair and flung her around in the foyer. Although she could use her speech to cry for help, she didn't. Her muteness was calming, and she wanted to stick with what she knew. Besides, that bitch didn't deserve to hear the sweet notes of her voice.

Instead of easing up, Wanda stole Juliette in the face so many times, her lips spewed blood. As if that wasn't enough, Wanda released her only for a second, to grab a pair of scissors that were on the counter. With them firmly in her hand, she lunged at Juliette.

"If you think you're going to take my husband away like the last bitch," she said, globs of spit falling out of her mouth, "then you have another thing coming. I will never let him go! Ever!"

This was all so confusing to Juliette. One minute Wanda said she loved her, and now this. Although Juliette had nothing but adoration in her heart for David, he had other thoughts as far as she was concerned. Secretly he was waiting for her to become of age, so that he could make his move. Although he cared about Wanda back in the day, she started letting herself go, and he was no longer sexually attracted to her. But Juliette...well Juliette was perfect in his eyes.

Wanda wasn't dumb when it came to her husband's affections for Juliette. She saw the beautiful diamond jewelry that David splurged on her, along with the beautiful clothing. But she hoped that her husband's love for the seventeen year old was pure, and that it would stay that way. That was until she cleaned her house thoroughly and saw a plastic bag under his side of the bed, in his gun case.

The moment she opened the bag, the first thing she smelled was the strong scent of another woman's vagina. When she looked inside, she saw fifteen pairs of Juliette's soiled underwear in assorted colors that he collected. Also inside of the bag was a stiff white rag, which was used to wipe the nut off of his hand, after he jerked off while smelling them.

While Wanda continues to wave the scissors like a mad woman, Juliette was able to push her away while she ran out of the front door. As she was doing so a Prince Georges County police officer was pulling up to the property. The next-door neighbor called them after hearing Wanda's crazed voice, thinking she was being murdered.

"Freeze," the officer yelled at Wanda holding a gun. He didn't know what she was about to do with those scissors, but he wasn't going to stop to find out either. "Don't move!"

She was standing over top of Juliette's bloodied body, until she saw the gun aimed in her direction.

"Put your hands in the air," the officer demanded.

Back to her senses, she dropped the scissors and said, "This is my home, and she tried to attack me." Although Juliette was clearly injured, Wanda didn't have a mark at all on her body.

"Who are you to her?"

"She's my foster child, and I'm taking care of her. I came home early and caught her trying to rob me," she lied. "When I walked into my room, she fought me. You should know that she is also mentally ill. You can ask her social worker, I have the number in my house. She doesn't speak or write. Now I need her taken out of my home immediately."

By this time, two more police officers arrived, and they all stepped out of their patrol cars, and with guns aimed and pointed at Juliette, due to automatically believing the story.

"Is it true," the officer asked Juliette.

"I said she can't speak," Wanda said hysterically. "What you asking her for?"

"Ma'am, we'll be the judge of that," he looked at Juliette and said, "Is it true? Can you or can you not speak?"

Juliette sniffled and in perfect English, and with a crisp tone said, "My name is Juliette Jamison, and this woman just tried to kill me."

Wanda was so frightened, believing like the foster care administration said that she couldn't talk, that she stood in shock.

"I am seventeen years old, and I am a minor. This woman found my underwear under her husband's bed, and she blames me for his infidelities. I am asking that you please help me, for I am in fear of my life."

After they investigated the scene, and found the bunch of underwear on the floor in the foyer, Juliette was immediately taken from the home. An investigation proved her story was correct, when it was discovered that as a teenager, David was a rapist. With the news of this discovery, David and Wanda's foster care licenses were revoked, and they were not allowed to ever care for another child again.

After that ordeal, Juliet realized that she could never put herself through another foster home. So after only two days in her new home, she ran away, and forged documents so that she could get a job at a fast food restaurant. With that job she was able to save up some money to buy a car. Although she was living at a shelter, until she could get on her feet, she was safer there than she was at any other foster home. She also immediately gave up her vow of silence.

And now, there she was, listening to her favorite singing group TLC, on the radio, as she drove down the street. The voice she kept away from the world for so long was now floating around in the car, as she sang along with the lyrics.

Although the dealer allowed her to take the car off of the lot, she still owed five hundred dollars, to settle the purchase price of a thousand bucks, they both agreed upon. Very reliable, she had the money in the purse she held in her hand.

When she strolled into Western Vision Motors, she smiled at all of the Greek dealers that were so helpful to her, as she made her way back to Ivan Hanno's office, to make the payment.

Western Vision Motors was a seedy business who's specialty included buying and selling cars to drug dealers. Although Western Vision Motors was also involved in the drug industry, they also made a great deal of money extorting the little guy like Juliette. They did this by selling them over priced automobiles, knowing they had little or no credit.

The moment Juliette walked through the door to his office, Ivan's dick hardened. Juliette's smooth brown skin, and long black loose curly hair, hung down her back. And the black long form fitting maxi dress she wore exposed the curves of her body. She was a knock-out.

"Hello, Juliette," he said walking around the desk with an extended clammy hand. "You enjoying that new car of yours?"

She lit up like the mother of a newborn baby. "Yes, sir." She shook his hand and released it, although he tried to hold onto it for a little longer. "It's everything I need for right now, and more. I thank you so much for the deal."

"Not a problem, have a seat," he motioned to the chair in front of his desk. "So what can I do for you to-day?"

Her chair squeaked softly. "I'm here to pay the last of my balance," she smiled. She reached into her purse and retrieved five hundred dollars from a bank envelope. She didn't have the money to give, but thankfully her good friend Garrick, who stayed with her at the shelter, thought enough of her to lend her the cash.

"Great," he said clapping his hands together. He reached in the desk and pulled out her file, without taking the money envelope. "That will be one thousand dollars."

Suddenly the arm that was extended, and holding the five hundred dollars felt heavy. "Ivan, there's been a mis-take. I owe you five hundred dollars." her hand dropped in her lap. "Remember, the entire price of the car was a thousand. I told you it was all I could raise, and you said it was fine, and that I could take the car off of the lot."

"I don't know about all that. Are you sure?"

"Yes, yes."

"Well let me check, beautiful, because the last thing I want to do is get over on you."

Although he scanned through the papers, he already knew what he was doing. There wasn't shit in those papers accept a bunch of game. After he finished reviewing absolutely nothing, he looked at Juliette who was waiting for a verdict. It was time to let her down easily, so that she could fall on his dick.

"I'm afraid you are mistaken, Juliette," he pointed at a place in the file. "I see right here that the balance owed is a thousand. With the total price of the car being fifteen hundred."

Juliet immediately felt sick to her stomach, and she was doing her best to keep her food down. It would be different if she just laid eyes on the car. But she already fell in love with it. After all, he allowed her to take it home, get it cleaned and everything. She even splurged on new car mats. Not to mention the fact that she just applied for a better job, that was further away from where she lived at the shelter. She would've never gone for that position, if she didn't have transportation.

"Ivan, I don't have that kind of money," she said softly. "Is there something else I can do for you?"

Yeah you can suck my dick. He thought.

"Like a payment plan or something?"

"I'm sorry, Juliette, but we don't do payment plans of that magnitude around here."

When she began to cry hysterically, and a few of the other dealers walked by his office, he got up and closed the door. They were all eager to come to her rescue, hoping that at the end of it all, she would end up in their beds. But that fish had been caught already, to hear Ivan tell it, and they could all kick rocks.

Ivan walked over to Juliette and rubbed her hair, "Stop crying, beautiful. I'm sure there's something we can do to work it out."

While she cried into her hands, he pulled his zipper down and released his dick. The uncircumcised mess, was already rock hard, and staring her in the face. In horror she looked up at him and he said, "If you really want that car, suck my dick and I'll give you that piece of shit for free."

"What?" she frowned. "I'm not doing that."

"Then I guess you never loved that car anyway."

When she looked at his dick, she considered what he wanted. From where she sat, she observed how the long black pubic hairs, surrounding his stiff white dick, were littered with what looked like a dried powdery substance. And how his dick hole, was already stuffed with white cream, like he fucked earlier that day, and didn't wash up. There was no way she was going to go through with it; she didn't care what he said. She was just about to tell him when someone interrupted the flow outside of the office.

"Alright, mothafuckas, you know what time it is, everybody on the floor," someone yelled outside of the closed door.

"What the fuck is happening?" Ivan said, due to being startled. Suddenly getting his dick sucked seemed so foolish.

When he placed his ear against the door, to see what was going on, it was kicked in on his face and a double barrel shot gun was aimed in his direction.

The gunman winked at Ivan and said, "Alright, baby boy, put that money under that desk on top of it. I came to make a withdrawal, and don't tell me you don't have it, because you know I know the deal."

Although Marcel Madison had yet to notice Juliette, she couldn't take her eyes off of him. Marcel's complexion was as chocolate as hers, but his hair was curly and blonde. He looked like he had been on the beach for days soaking up the sun, which left him with a bronzed tan. She'd never seen a black man with a glow like his before and he looked as if he just stepped out of a *Visit Brazil* ad. He was perfect.

"I can't believe you doing me like this," Ivan said, "as many cars as I sold to you. This is how you repay me?"

"Fuck you, Greek, you been getting over on niggas for the past twenty years. It's time to render to me. Now get my money, quick, because you testing my patience right now."

As Marcel observed Ivan gather his money, he suddenly realized that his pants were open. When he looked to his left, he was staring into the face of the most beautiful woman he'd ever seen in his life. Although it wasn't the time or the place, he couldn't help but wink at her anyway.

And then something dawned on him. Ivan was up to his old tricks. When Marcel realized what was happening, since Ivan had his pants down, and she was sitting down, he grew angry. Ivan pulled the same slick shit on a good friend of his, not too long ago and he never forgot. Ivan told his friend the car was one amount, and when she bought back the rest of the money, after he allowed her to leave the lot with the car, he said she owed more. As an alternative he offered her his dick, which she refused.

"So you up to the same shit ain't you? Hustling black women out of their money, for them piece of shit cars out back?"

"What you talking about man, I—"

When Ivan tried to move for the gun he had strapped under the desk, Marcel awarded him by blasting a hole into his forearm, severing it in half. Ivan dropped to the floor and screamed out in pain, his bone fragments resting on the floor below him.

"Don't let the pretty face fool you, Greek, I'ma gangsta."

"The money is all there, everything, please don't shoot me anymore!"

Marcel focused on Juliette. "Hey"— he took the navy blue book bag off of his back, and tossed it into her lap— "how 'bout you stack the money into that bag for me."

The moment he addressed her, Juliette stood up like a soldier in the military. She didn't understand what she was feeling, because she was scared and turned on at the same time. Maybe it was the fact that before moving to America, she was the citizen of the most dangerous city in the world. Or, maybe she wasn't afraid because something told her that Marcel would change her life forever.

Juliette placed stack after stack in the bag, and when she was done she stood behind Marcel who was still aiming at Ivan. "Thanks, beautiful," he said winking at her. "Hey, Ivan, I think I'm gonna take the girl and the money too, now we not gonna have hard feelings after this are we?"

He looked up at him from the floor and angrily mouthed, "What do you think, nigger?"

"I figured as much," Marcel replied, before splattering his brains all over the wall behind him.

"Let's be out," Marcel said as he entered the sales floor, after leaving Ivan's office.

When Juliette followed him, it looked like a massacre had occurred. Blood and gore was all over the cars on the showroom floor, and every dealer who was alive earlier was now resting in peace.

Marcel ran out of the dealership and Juliette was right on his heels. Marcel, along with his men, piled into an all black van that was waiting outside. When everyone was inside the van pulled off.

"Dank, you checked the repair shop's safe too right?" Marcel asked a short teenager with a baldhead, as he sat down. Juliette sat so close to him, the right side of her ass wasn't touching the seat.

"You know it, boss." he raised a black bag stuffed with bills. "You were right," he put it down, "the safe was behind the tires, but we got 'em."

"My, man!" Marcel grinned snatching the bag.

Juliette sat quietly as she watched all seven of his goons remove their masks. There were six men, and one female. She felt at home around them, and part of her felt bad about this.

"You coming with me right?" Marcel asked, breaking her out of her thoughts. "I got a feeling if you do, I will change your life forever."

His words gave her chills, and she wondered how did he know she was thinking the same thing.

Three hours later Marcel parked the van in a hidden garage, and was driving Juliette home in his beautiful white Mercedes Benz, E-Class. She couldn't believe how gorgeous his car was, but more importantly how good he looked driving it.

Fifteen minutes later when they pulled up at their destination, and Marcel saw that she lived at a shelter, he parked his car and looked over at her.

He rubbed his hands together. "So what's your name, beautiful?"

She giggled, realizing that she'd been with him since the robbery, and they knew nothing about each other. "Juliette."

His eyebrows rose. "Like the story, Romeo and Juliette?"

"Just like the story," she replied.

"That's a dope ass name, your mama knew what she was doing didn't she?"

"I never met my mother," she lied, looking into her lap.

He looked at the shelter again. "What you want out of life?"

"To survive." She remembered what her mother said. To always be perfecting her survival instincts.

"Anything else?" he asked.

"I want to be a writer, but nobody wants to read the work of an unknown. That's always been a dream of mine."

"Do you think you can have those things, by living here?"

"No." she looked out of the window, and at the shelter's door. "But it's the safest place I know."

Garrick, her only other friend in the world was standing outside of it waiting. He had been worried sick about her, ever since he heard about the massacre that had taken place at Western Vision Motors.

35

Marcel reached into the bag and gave her the three thousand dollars he promised, for her part in the heist. Sure it was more than he needed to give, but he was testing her, to see what kind of woman she was.

"It's like this, Juliette, you can keep that money, which will buy you a short start in life. Or, I can put that money back in my bag, and you can come with me, and help me spend the whole eighty thousand. What you gonna do?"

"But I don't even know you," she said, trying not to look into his eyes. His gaze was hypnotic.

"But here you are, alone in a car, with a cold blooded murderer anyway." he placed his hand softly on her face. "And yet you aren't even scared."

Her heart thumped softly in her chest.

"Come with me, Juliette, and let me take care of you like I know I can. I promise that you'll never meet another mothafucka like me. Don't blow this shit. You want this life, I can tell."

She looked out of the window at Garrick, and felt torn, because she knew he loved her, even if she didn't love him back. He was extremely attractive too, with his dark chocolate skin and thick wavy hair. Although she never told him before, she had given some serious thought about being with him like he asked her once a week. Besides, Garrick did more for her in the shelter than any man had in her entire life, even though she never once fucked him.

Just the other day she learned that he was moving out, and getting his own place in a month. He asked her to come with him, and she was contemplating telling him yes. But now, everything changed.

"What's your name?"

"Marcel," he said.

"Okay, Marcel, give me one second." She peeled five hundred dollars off of the stack, got out of the car and walked over to Garrick. "Here's the money I owe you."

"I don't want your money, Juliette," he said looking into her eyes. "I want you."

"But I want a different life. A better life than you can't give me right now."

He looked over at her shoulder, at the beautiful white car parked in the front. "He'll hurt you if you go with him. I know his kind. And I want you to know that I would never hurt you."

"It may be true, but it's a chance I'm willing to take." She walked backwards toward the car, keeping her eyes on Garrick the entire time. Finally she eased back into the car and closed the door softly. She waved goodbye to him.

"Is he going to be a problem?"

"Not since I chose you."

He winked and pulled off.

"Good, and just so you know, from here on out I'm going to call you *Jewels*. You cool with that?"

"If you treat me right you can call me whatever you want."

When Marcel pulled up at an old brick apartment building in Washington DC, Juliette was a little thrown off. She didn't know where she expected him to live, but it certainly wasn't in an apartment.

When they walked inside Marcel said, "You can put your stuff over there." He pointed at a small couch.

The one bedroom apartment was neat, but real tight. Boxes of expensive tennis shoes were lined up along the walls in the living room, and the apartment didn't appear to have too much more space inside.

Marcel grabbed her hand and led her to the bedroom, where his mother was already in the bed sleep. Across from her bed was another queen size bed where he slept.

Confused about what was going on, she followed his lead, and jumped out of her clothes like he did. She kept on her panties and bra, and climbed under the covers with him.

"I'm a virgin, Marcel," she told him.

He laughed. "I can tell. I've been with enough women to know."

Partially relieved she said, "Marcel, what's going on?" She laid her head on his chest. Although they just met, it was like she always belonged to him.

He fluffed the pillow behind his head. "What do you mean," he asked, rubbing her hair, eager to get some sleep.

"Why are you living here? In the apartment," she whispered. "With your mother?"

"Because I like staying with moms I guess."

"This doesn't add up. I mean, I just saw you take more money than I'd ever seen in my life, and I can tell by the way you held the gun, that it wasn't your first time."

"True," he said, yawning.

"Well how come you sleeping in the same room with your mother, in a one bedroom apartment at that? When you can find an apartment of your own?"

He looked over at her. "It's like this, I make a lot of money, but I'm not good on managing it. So I see a bunch of dough but I throw it up in the air, and can never keep it long enough to move out. Who knows," he shrugged. "Maybe you can help me manage my paper, and help get me out of here. You know, everything happens for a reason."

CHAPTER 3

In The Courtroom:

"So after you met your husband at the taco truck, were you faithful?" the prosecutor asked.

"He wasn't my husband during the time we worked at the truck together," She said shuffling in her seat.

Juliette knew that she could not reveal that her husband was an armed robber, because they would question why she stayed with him. She also didn't want to be linked up with any of Marcel's past crimes. If she was going to be found not guilty, she needed to remain calm and pick and choose what she would tell them. She needed to control the situation.

"Well did you sleep with other men, during your relationship? Before the marriage?"

"What, of course not," she yelled widening her eyes.

"Did you sleep with other women, during the course of your relationship?"

How the fuck did they find that out? She thought.

"I loved my husband, more than anything in the world and I would never be unfaithful. And that goes for men and women too."

● ● ●

The Truth:
Spring, 1999

It was Jewles' first day of class and it had been a long day. All she wanted to do was kick back in the beautiful apartment she shared with Marcel, in an upscale part of Washington DC, and relax.

Marcel had proven to be everything she needed. When she needed clothing, he bought it for her. When she wanted particular furniture, he paid for it. When she wanted to go to community college, since her grades weren't good enough for any other university, since she purposely flunked out before admitting that she could read and write, he paid for her to get a GED. And she was then able to take college courses. Marcel was on point. She didn't have to do anything but understand that he loved his profession, and would never change for anyone or anybody.

As she walked into their apartment, she was thrown off when she saw a red silk bra by the door, with the matching underwear thrown over the edge of her imported Italian cream sofa. But where was the person they belonged to?

Confused, she closed and locked her door, and threw her book bag on the floor. When she opened the door to her bedroom, she saw a set of brown female legs wrapped around Marcel's waist. While another beautiful white Italian woman, with long dark brown hair, sat on a chair and taped the sex act.

Her voice was stuck in her throat and she was paralyzed. Even if he was doing his thing, did he have to bring them back to their home? "Marcel," Jewels said softly walking closer to the bed, "what's going on here?" She scanned the room, and the sweet smell of perfume and sex filled the air.

He jumped up and hid his chest with the sheet, exposing the beautiful woman under him. "Baby, this is my best friend Gia Apa," he said pointing at the tall Italian woman with the camera. "And this is Ursula, my other closest friend."

"Marcel, I don't understand, I mean, I thought we were in a committed relationship." Her face was calm but her heart was pounding.

"We are, it's just that, I mean...I thought you were supposed to be in school anyway. What are you doing here?"

"This is wrong, Marcel, why would you do this to me? All I did was try and love you." Her eyes began to water, but she didn't give them permission to release the flood.

"Jewels, please don't tell me you 'bout to cry. You the first bitch I ever put up in an apartment before, chill out. I'm me, and I'm going to always be that way. I thought you understood that shit!"

Hearing the irritation in his voice, Jewels quickly assessed the situation. She saw their clothing thrown across her room, and felt a bowl of pain form in her stomach. But she made a decision in that moment and it was crystal. Marcel was her nigga, and she was not about to sit on the sidelines, and allow someone else to take him from her, simply because she was being a prude.

Instead Jewels stood in the middle of the bedroom floor, and lowered the zipper to her tight blue jeans. She pushed them to her ankles, before wiggling out of her pink panties, and throwing them on the floor too.

"Baby, what you doing," he asked, viewing her strip tease.

She ignored him. Instead of speaking she removed her red sweatshirt, exposing her bra.

Marcel could do nothing but smile. All his life he was a cheater. He used women as he saw fit and didn't care what they thought about it. But there he was, looking at Jewels' naked body, knowing that essentially she was saying that I am ready to take you just as you are, and I don't care what I have to do.

Turned on, he stood up and met her in the middle of the floor. He slowly brought her to the bed, as if she were fragile, and in the throws of changing her mind. Ursula's perky breasts stood at attention, as she opened her arms to welcome Jewels. Although Jewels was nervous at first, eventually she melted into her warm body, and relaxed the moment Ursula placed her soft lips against hers, and she tasted the minty sweetness of her breath.

With their lips pressed together, Ursula stiffened her tongue, and Jewels sucked it softly, and then harder like it was a dick. Their breasts mashed together, and Jewels could feel the warmth of Ursula's pussy against her waist. Wanting to feel her wetness, but without removing her kiss, Jewels raised her body so that both of their pussies were touching. In the moment she imagined that she was Marcel, and that she was now fucking Ursula. When she felt her clit rubbing against Ursula's, she maneuvered her hips so that their pussies could grind harder. All sorts of tingling sensations took over Jewels' body as she breathed in the sweet smell of Ursula's pussy.

Just when it couldn't get any better, Jewels felt her man's warm chest press against her back. While the women kissed, Marcel gently suckled Jewels' earlobe, before running his warm tongue along the line of her neck. Jewels was so wet now, that her pussy juice poured over Ursula's like a fountain.

Which is why when Marcel pushed his stiff dick into Jewels' body, her body trembled. Throughout Jewels' seventeen years, she had dodged predators and lustful men, to save her body for the right person. Marcel was that man. And although the first time they made love, about a month ago danced in her mind, it couldn't touch the sensuality of this moment.

"Damn, Jewels, baby, why that pussy so wet," Marcel asked banging her softly from behind. "This thing feels as hot as an oven."

"Is it real wet, Marcel," Ursula asked, looking up at him.

"How about you check it out for yourself," he suggested.

Taking his advice, slowly Ursula eased her finger into Jewels' tight warm pussy. Jewels' walls tightened, and her syrup poured all over Ursula's finger. When her digit was coated with cream, she removed it and saw her finger glistening. But when she sucked Jewels' juice off like it was icing on a cake, Jewels' was beyond turned on.

Extra horny, Jewels kissed Ursula passionately again, as the love of her life continued to bang her from behind. Now she was really feeling the moment, and there was no turning back.

Although Marcel had many threesomes in his lifetime, this one was the best ever, because he was really feeling Jewels. Marcel, who couldn't handle it anymore, pulled out of Jewels and said, "Ursula, come lick my baby clean." He was trying to prolong his orgasm for as long as possible.

Ursula greedily positioned herself between Jewels' legs, while Marcel fucked Ursula in the asshole. Even Gia had placed the camera down, and took to fingering her pussy as she watched the show.

Jewels was in ecstasy, and did not want the moment to end. Ever. They didn't stop until each of them had reached two orgasms a piece.

After that night, every week the four of them got together and played the freaky game. Ursula had become a staple in Jewels' and Marcel's lives, and Jewels welcomed her and loved when she was around. She was affectionate, warm and even nourished her dreams to become a writer.

There was nothing about Ursula that was jealous hearted, although Jewels couldn't say the same thing for his best friend Gia. Unlike Ursula, Jewels always got the impression that Gia, who was money hungry, would try and steal Marcel from her if the opportunity ever presented itself. This alone kept Jewels on top of her game at all times.

A month later, when it was time to rob another dealership, which also specialized in washing drug money, Marcel suggested that Jewels come along. Before doing the heist, Jewels, along with Marcel, Gia and six other members of Marcel's gang, sat in the living room to discuss the plan. They went over the operation to hit Red Diamond Motors in Virginia so that they could be on the same page.

"Our inside track said there are five safes," Marcel said. "Right here, here, here, here, and here," he pointed at the paper, and then looked up at all of them. "If we do this right, we gonna be set for a minute. This is the big one. And from what I'm told, they sitting on no less than two hundred thousand at any given time," Marcel coached. "So let's do this shit!"

As Marcel and his gang were inside of the dealership, Jewels sat in the van, behind the steering wheel, quivering. There was one thing on her mind. And it was that the Lord, bring back both Marcel and Ursula safely. The two people she had come to love deeply.

When the gang members finally got back into the van, with their weapons smelling of gunpowder and smoke, Jewels didn't breathe until she saw Marcel and Ursula's faces.

"Oh my, God, I'm so happy to see ya'll," Jewels said excitedly. She moved from behind the steering wheel and passionately kissed Marcel first, and then Ursula on the lips second. When she was done she got behind the steering wheel and got them away from the scene.

Marcel was right about that gig, because the hit netted them over two hundred thousand dollars. When the money was divided later that night amongst his crew, Marcel, Ursula and Jewels went back to their apartment to make love on a bed of one hundred dollar bills. Jewels loved Marcel, and more than anything she wanted to be his wife. His love for her, coupled with Ursula's attention, made her feel complete in the relationship. She could see herself with both of them for life.

After they finished fucking that night, Marcel left Jewels and got on the phone to talk to his best friend Gia. While in the living room, Jewels could hear him going on and on, about how he successfully led his team to the major victory.

After five minutes of realizing he wasn't returning to the bed, Jewels crawled up under the covers with Ursula, and rested her face on her belly. Although Ursula was screaming her name about thirty minutes earlier, now she seemed distant.

"What's wrong, Ursula, I see something behind your eyes," Jewels said looking up to her. "You feel okay?"

"How come you're the only one in the world who knows when something is wrong with me?" She asked running her fingers through Jewels' hair.

She shrugged. "I don't know, I guess it's because I care," she said softly.

"My boyfriend proposed, and he wants to move me to Atlanta," she sighed. "And I'm thinking about saying yes." Although Jewels remained silent, Ursula could feel her rapid heartbeat against her thigh, and she rubbed her hair a little firmer to calm her down. She knew Jewels was devastated about losing her, and she felt the same. "Don't worry, Jewels, because no matter where I am, I will forever love you. Plus I'm just a phone call away if you need me."

Jewels looked up at her. "You love me for real?"

"I truly do," Ursula said, with a tear rolling down her face. "And I want to tell you something that's very important." She looked through the open doorway to be sure Marcel hadn't gotten off of the phone. "You have to always think one step ahead of Marcel. I know he cares about you, I swear I do, but he's a man of circumstance. He'll do whatever you allow him to so you have to set your limits, and force him to honor them, Jewels. Always remember that or his love will kill you."

Ursula moved to Atlanta, and Jewels called her almost everyday, although she never answered the phone. Jewels never saw Ursula after that day, but her words lived on in her heart forever. If only she would have listened to her then, she wouldn't be facing a murder wrap now.

CHAPTER 4

In The Courtroom:

Adele Abigail walked up to her client who was sitting on the stand. Her beauty was almost as intoxicating as her young defendant. "Juliette, was Marcel a good man?"

Juliette wiped her tears with the ball of tissue in her hand. "No, not all of the time, although I think sometimes he tried."

"What do you mean? Be clearer."

"He was only good, when he felt like being that way. Otherwise he was just evil," she said truthfully. "And there was no use in telling him how I felt about anything, because his mind was always made up. I hated that about him."

"Elaborate more," Adele said.

Juliette looked at the judge who nodded for her to continue. Then she focused on her attorney. "When he got the mind to, or was frustrated, sometimes he beat me."

Adele approached her client carefully. Her high heels clicking sounded like a soft beat. "Are you telling the court that Marcel was abusive?"

Juliette remained silent.

The Truth:
Spring, 2000

♪ *Oooooo that dress so scandalous, and you know another nigga can't handle this.* ♪

Juliette was in the passenger seat listening to her favorite new song, *The Thong Song*, by Sisqo', as Marcel drove them to a carryout. Although she tried to be in a good mood, Marcel was angry that a robbery he just participated only three hours earlier, was unsuccessful. He was on the phone talking to his protégé, about the matter.

"Aight, Dank, you gotta be more careful"— he turned the music down despite Jewels singing along with the lyrics—"this is the last time you can make a dumb ass move like that, slim! I mean had Gia not banged that nigga who was walking up behind you, you could've been dead. I'm talking about brains splattered over the cars in the lot type of dead."

"You right, boss, you right. I'm gonna be careful next time, I just got confused."

"Well I'm tired of hearing that shit," he said. "If I didn't fuck with you, we wouldn't even be having this conversation right now!"

"I know, man, I know. And I'm sorry this job came up dry, but I know we going to do better next time. It's going to be a big pay day I can feel it."

After a few more useless words from his comrade, Marcel hung up on him, and pulled up to the restaurant. Irritated with Dank he took his problems out on his girl instead.

"Last night when we was fucking, I smelled your pussy," he parked the car in front of the carryout. "That better never happen again."

49

She looked over at him, trying to figure out the best way to voice her opinion. She learned a few things from Marcel as time went by, and one of them was to never say exactly what was on her mind, especially when he was angry. So she orchestrated her tone and words carefully.

"Marcel, I was on my period," she said softly, looking over at him. "What you smelled was blood, and I'm sorry it bothered you. Remember, I told you that I didn't want to fuck you right then, and you told me to open my fucking legs anyway?"

"Then the next time you open your legs, and you on your period, you better clean your blood first, bitch," he cracked his knuckles. "Because if I ever smell anything like that coming out of your body again"— he pointed in her face— "I'll kill you with my bare hands."

Jewels didn't feel much like arguing with him. Besides, she'd taken an hour-long bath before they made love so she knew she was fresh as she could be. He was just mad at the world and using her as his punching bag. They had a long day, and all she wanted was to go into the house and grab some shut-eye.

"Whatever you say, Marcel."

"Yeah, I know that already, bitch," he said rolling his eyes. "What you want to eat out here again?"

"I'll take a steak and cheese, with everything on it," she sighed soft enough not to annoy him.

He got out of the car, and fifteen minutes later returned with his order, which was correct, and hers, which was all, fucked up. "Marcel," she said opening the silver wrapper and observing the sandwich. "I asked for a steak and cheese, this is a fried chicken and cheese sandwich." She raised it up.

"So," he said turning the car back on. "Eat that mothafucka and fall back."

"So," she repeated sarcastically. "I don't want this shit, Marcel. I hate fried chicken sandwiches, you know that."

"Jewels, you eat steak and cheese subs all the time, for once in your life eat something different."

"Well I eat steak and cheese subs because I love them, Marcel. If I wanted a chicken and cheese sandwich I would have asked you for it. This not fair, I mean your food right, what about mine?"

Marcel turned the car off, threw his sandwich in the backseat like a football and then turned around to face her. "Who the fuck are you talking too?" His fists clenched before him.

"You know what"— she threw her hands up — "it don't even matter, just take me home. I'll make something when I get there." She wrapped the sandwich back up, and faced the road ahead of her.

And the moment her eyes were off of him, Marcel hit her in the face so hard with a closed fist that her head knocked against the window. Jewels was temporarily delirious, because she never expected him to treat her so violently. Sure they had their beefs in the past, and he may have grabbed her by the arm, or snatched her by the shoulders to get her attention for bully's sake. But he never did anything like this before.

And then to add physical insult to injury, instead of asking if she was okay he said, "Get the fuck out of my car, Jewels, before I really hurt you up in here. I don't even want to be around you."

She held onto her face. "Marcel, what is going on, baby?" she said softly. "I mean I know you never meant to hurt me, and I know you're mad that the heist didn't work out as planned, but you never punished me like this before. Why would you do that?"

"Bitch, did you hear what the fuck I just said? I don't care about how you feel! Get the fuck out my car, before I lay serious hands on you. You got five seconds or what I'm going to do next will place you down for good."

"Marcel, please I—"

When she disobeyed him, he punched her in the stomach, and her mouth flew open. "If you make me hit you again, you're going to need a paramedic." He pointed at the door. "Get the fuck out of my car!"

Jewels pulled up the handle, and rolled out of the car. The moment she closed the door, he sped off, leaving her in the middle of the street confused and alone. Jewels watched until the Mercedes Benz emblem on Marcel's ride, faded into the night.

It wasn't until he was gone that she realized that she didn't have her purse, phone or a dime to her name. Not to mention the fact that she didn't have anyone to call. Marcel was her world, and her only family. If he abandoned her now, since she didn't have any money saved, she would be back to where she started before he met her. Out on the streets or in a shelter.

With nothing else to do, Jewels walked an hour in one direction, on the same road, hoping Marcel would have pity and turn back around, to scoop her up. It never happened. Before long the darkness of the night covered her, and she found herself sitting on the curb, outside of a motel crying. She could also smell rain coming.

"Wait a minute," a stranger said walking up to her, "what is a beautiful thing like you doing out here crying? Whoever hurt you, must not know what he gave up."

She wiped her tears away and looked up at him. He was a tall black older man, with kind eyes and a river of gray hair, running around the back of his head, from ear to ear.

"It's a long story," she sniffled. "I really don't want to talk about it now."

When the rain began to pour heavily on her, she fell deeper into depression.

"Do you have somewhere to go, child?"

"No," she admitted.

"I have a daughter your age, and I would be devastated if someone didn't help her. Now I'm staying in this motel tonight"— he pointed at the run down building behind him— "because my flight was delayed and is not going out until the morning. There's only one bed, but you're welcome to stay with me. I won't try anything if you're worried. You can also use the phone if you need to make some calls. If I had a car I would take you to where you have to go, but I don't."

"How do I know you won't try something?"

"Because you're beautiful, but you're much younger than the women I'm attracted to." he pulled out his wallet. "Besides this is a picture of my wife, and we've been married for fifty years. Trust me when I say you're safe with me."

Jewels stood up and observed the picture. He looked so comfortable and in love with his wife, and she immediately trusted him and let her guards down. She knew she was taking a chance, but what else was she going to do? If she hitchhiked home, Marcel might be angry with her, and finish her off. This old man was her only hope, and as odd as it was, she was grateful for him.

So she walked up the stairs behind him, in an effort to get out of the rain, and get her mind together.

When she finally got to the room she said, "Can I make a call?"

He took his wet shirt off and said, "Sure, help your-self." he handed her the phone in the room, and walked into the bathroom.

Everything inside of the room looked drab, and it made her miss the luxury apartment she shared with Marcel even more. *Why are you doing me like this, ba-by? I love you so much.* She thought.

Jewels called Marcel several times, to see if he had calmed down, and would allow her to return home, but he didn't answer. When it was obvious that he was done with her, she called the only other number she remem-bered. The phone rang five times before his voice lit up the phone.

"Hello, Garrick, I know you don't want to hear from me," she sat on the edge of the bed, and it squeaked loud-ly. "But it's me, Jewels."

"Jewels?" he asked.

Remembering that Jewels was the nickname Marcel had given to her, and he wasn't familiar with it, she said, "I'm sorry, it's me, Juliette."

"Baby, oh my God, where are you? Do you know how much I worry about you? I'm always calling the shelter to see if you are there, but hoping you don't show up because I want better for you, even though I want to hear your voice. Juliette, I'm so happy you remembered my number."

Just hearing his voice, and knowing that someone cared about her, made her feel a little better. It made her feel loved, and worthy. "Garrick, I'm doing badly, really badly right now."

The old man walked out of the bathroom, wearing only his pants and no shirt. Thick gray hairs crawled all over his chest, making him look weird. She took her eyes off of him, in case he thought she wanted him in some way.

"Come to LA, baby, please. I'm doing well out here now, and I can take care of you. I have a new job as a paralegal, and I'm taking classes to become a lawyer. If you give me some time, I'll be very wealthy."

"I don't know, Garrick," she said looking at her fingers. "LA is just so far away."

"Please, just think about it, Juliette, because I adore you. And I know you with that nigga, out there doing God knows what, but he will never love you like I do. He will never appreciate what it means to take care of a woman like you. Juliette, you've been through a lot, a whole lot, and I can hear it in your voice. It's your time to relax. Let me love you, baby. Please. You can't see me but I'm on my knees, begging you."

When the old man walked toward her, he looked at her and said, "I'll be out of your way in a minute." She covered the phone so that Garrick couldn't hear his weird voice. "Do you want anything? I'm going to McDonalds?"

"No, I'll be fine," she said covering the phone tighter. She watched him walk out of the door, and placed the headset to her ear again. "Garrick, are you still there?"

"Yes, baby, I am. Are you okay?"

"I'm fine," she sighed.

"Are you going to let me take care of you? Like I know I can?"

"Yes, I will come to you," she laughed.

"When?" he asked excitedly.

"I'll call you tomorrow to give you the place that I'll be, and if you can send me the plane ticket to go to LA, that will be good," she said playing with the phone cord.

"I will, Juliette, and I want you to know that you're making the right decision too."

Jewels said her goodbyes to him and climbed into the uncomfortable bed. Ten minutes later the old man returned, smelling like French Fries and her stomach growled. Suddenly she realized what a mistake it was to not ask for something to eat. She closed her eyes, when the bed was weighted down on the left. Instead of him lying down, he ate the food for twenty minutes.

Ten minutes later, the lights went out and she closed her eyes tighter. She didn't want him thinking that anything would be kicking off between them. When he finally got into the bed with her, she could smell the meat from his sandwich, along with his ashy breath. He wiggled closer, and the moist heat from his nostrils brushed against her nape.

He wrestled a little with something down low, and then she felt his stiff dick press against the middle of her jeans. She held onto her breath and allowed him to poke her with it repeatedly, as he jerked off. She thought about what she already knew. Everything he was saying about having a daughter like her, and a wife he cared about, was just a ploy to get her into his motel room, and into the bed. The sad thing is it worked.

"Mmmmm," he moaned, as he quickly rubbed his dick against her jeans. "Mmmmmm, yes, you sexy young bitch."

When she felt a quick jitter, and heard a harsh moan, she could feel his warm liquid shoot out of his dick and spill onto her jeans. She slammed her eyes tighter, and kept them closed, until the sun shined through the windows, telling her it was okay to start her life over, in a new state. In a new place.

Quickly Jewels stood up, and looked at the back of her cum stained jeans in the mirror. When she looked at the bed, at his ugly face, he was still sleep. She didn't care though, because this would be the last time she would have to disrespect herself again. Her life was changing because that morning, she was throwing away her love for Marcel and starting all over fresh with Garrick.

But when she stepped out of the motel room, she saw Marcel standing out front, next to his Benz, with a look of regret upon his face.

She left the door slightly ajar, stepped closer to the railing, and looked down at him. She wasn't sure if she needed to run back into the room for safety or what. She was confused. After all, he gut punched her earlier.

So many questions ran through her mind. How did he know she was there? "Marcel, what...what are you doing here?"

He slowly walked up the steps, and towards her. "Jewels, I fucked up, baby. I should've never put my hands on you. I mean, you know that shit with not making out on the money I thought we should have, fucked me up. *Majorly.* By the time I realized what I'd done to you, you were long gone."

"How did you find me, Marcel?"

"Jewels," he laughed stepping up to her, and taking her hands into his own, "come on, baby, you mean after all this time you still don't know what kind of nigga you with? I'm money, sweetheart. Naw, scratch that, I'm money, power and respect. That means I know all and see more. How the fuck you think my bitch gonna be anywhere in DC, and my people not let me know about it?"

This scared her, because she thought about Garrick, and the fact that she was about to leave him. Could he find her in LA too?

"I didn't do anything," she said looking at the open door, to be sure it was still open so that she could dodge inside if he struck her again, "with anybody. It wasn't even like that."

"I know." he rubbed her shoulders. "But how about you go get into the car so that I can take you home, and I'll be down in a minute."

She walked closely to the stairs, and stopped before walking down them. "Where you going, Marcel?"

"Jewels, go to the car," he pointed to his shiny Benz. "You know I'm not going to tell you again right. Do you want me to punish you more?"

"No, I'm leaving now."

She obeyed his orders, not trying to rock the boat. Right before she climbed into the car she heard a series of gunfire sounding off in the motel room.

CHAPTER 5

In The Courtroom:

Jewels sat in the stand, after just talking about how Marcel beat her shamelessly for wanting the right food order, from the carryout. Although she was being truthful then, she didn't tell them about the old man from the motel, or that Marcel killed him. She had to keep some things secret, to prevent them from knowing about the bodies, and crimes they experienced together and apart.

"That sounds pretty bad," Adele said, "I'm sure it must've been hard not having support, and being left out on that street alone, until the next morning when he picked you up. By the way what time did he return?"

"About, five in the morning."

"Can you ever think of a time where he was good to you?" Adele continued.

Juliette pulled the records about their relationship up in her mind, the one she went over with her attorney. She knew if she didn't tell them something good about him, the jury might never believe her. After all, who marries a man who is totally evil?

"I can remember one time," she said.

"Do you mind telling the court about that day?"

The Truth:

Summer, 2001

Juliette was in bed, shivering as the radio played in the background. She had chills all over her body, and as usual Marcel was nowhere to be found. Lately she was starting to realize that although she was in a relationship with Marcel, she was still alone, and it hurt badly.

All he wanted to do was run the streets, with his best friend Gia. Sometimes he even stayed out all night, and when she would ask him to come home, he'd threaten to put her out for hassling him. She was lost and starting to feel hate brewing up in her heart.

"We have a breaking story," the radio host announced. Although Jewels was feeling bad, she focused on his voice and the news. *"We want to inform you that the singer Aaliyah has died today in a plane crash. As details continue to come in, we'll keep you posted. In Aaliyah's remembrance we will play her music all day."*

The first song they played was *If Your Girl Only Knew*. The news of Aaliyah's death stabbed her in the heart, and made her feel even worse. Now not only was she sick, one of her favorite singers just died, and Marcel was not home. She was about to go make herself some soup, when Marcel strolled into the bedroom.

He had a Gucci book bag flung over one side of his arm. He tossed it to the floor by the door. "Baby, baby, did you hear about Aaliyah?" he walked deeper into the room, removed his watch and wallet, and threw it onto the dresser. He did this all without even looking at her face. "She died in an airplane crash."

Jewels didn't respond, instead she remained in the bed shivering. So he turned around and looked at his silent girlfriend.

"Baby, what's wrong?" he sat on the edge of the bed, and rubbed the sweaty damp hair stuck on her face. "You look terrible."

"I'm sick, Marcel," she said, rolling her eyes. "I think I have a fever or something."

He flipped his hand over, and felt the heat of her body via her forehead. His eyes widened when he felt the warmth of her face. "Oh my, God, baby, you have a fever. How that happen?"

"I figured I had a temperature," she said lightly. "I was walking around and the next thing I knew I was too weak to stand up, so I been in bed."

"Don't worry because I'm here now," he said. He removed his jacket and walked into the bathroom. When he returned he had a thermometer in his hand. "Open your mouth," he said. She did. He took her temperature and it was 105. "Jewels, we gotta bring that temperature down. Damn, I didn't know you were in here sick, why didn't you tell me?"

"I called you the other day—"

"You didn't say anything about you being sick," he interrupted, after placing the thermometer on the side table.

"Because I didn't think you cared."

"Jewels, I might do my shit out on the streets, but if I would've known you was in here on the half, I would've come home. I'm fucked up in the head that you don't know that. I ain't that bad."

Marcel rushed back into the bathroom, and filled the tub up with cool water. He also poured alcohol under the running water. When he was done he went back into the bedroom, lifted Jewels in his arms, and sat her on the toilet. Slowly he peeled her clothes off, while Aaliyah's greatest hits sang in the background on the radio. When her beautiful naked body was exposed, he raised her and slowly placed her into the water.

"Marcel, it's so cold," she shivered as he cupped pockets of water with his hand, and poured it all over her body.

"I know, baby, I know, but I gotta bring your temperature down." He looked into her eyes, deeply, and Jewels could feel the love he had for her. He wasn't just doing something to make himself look good. In that moment, he really wanted her well.

Carefully, and gently he continued to wipe her down with chilled water, and when he was done, he dressed her into her favorite warm pink cotton pajamas. After dressing her and changing the bedding to fresh sheets, he placed her in the bed and rushed back out of the apartment. He did so without mentioning to her where he was going.

In Jewels' mind, she just knew that he was leaving her again to hit the streets. Instead he came back with fresh fruit, and a fruit juice maker. Marcel spent an hour in the kitchen pressing fresh orange juice for her, and when he was finished, and covered in orange pulp, he came back with a half full glass of juice.

"Here, baby, get this up in you."

Marcel bought her a lot of material things, but up to that point, him making that juice was the most romantic thing that he'd ever done in their relationship. He not only wanted her to get better, but he also wanted her to know that he cared, and she felt it.

After she drank the juice, he took his clothes off and climbed into the bed behind her. His warm chest pressed against her back and she could feel his love. It was electrifying. Here she was, thinking this man didn't care, and now she could feel his silent prayers for her wellbeing.

"Do you know that the first day I saw you, I knew you would be my wife," Marcel whispered in her ear. "I wasn't even going to hit that dealership that day, because I knew Ivan knew my face. But the moment I saw you, I knew why I allowed Dank to talk me into it."

"I know you wanted to be with me, but I thought I would be your lawfully wedded wife."

"This is better, Jewels, and one day you going to understand why." He paused "Because I've never been with anybody on this level. And I know things aren't going the way you want them to, but I want you to stick with me, because I love you. Do you believe me?"

"I believe you, Marcel, I finally feel it. I mean you put me up in an apartment, bought me everything I needed, and I've always appreciated you for that."

He pulled her closer to him. "Jewels, you can't die on me." He whispered into her neck, his warm breath tickling her softly. "I don't know why you sick, but you gotta get better." She could feel the fear in his voice that she would leave him.

"What?" she said softly. "Who said anything about dying?"

"After hearing that Aaliyah died, and seeing you in here with the fever, it made me realize how much you mean to me."

Jewels felt all sorts of tingling sensations occur all over her body. Marcel was everything to her, and each day she prayed for the day that he would ask her to be his wife, and now she was feeling like it was really possible.

"Marcel, I love you so much, and as long as you continue to love me back, that will never change, and I will never leave you. I'm not going anywhere, and neither are you. We were born for each other, and I sincerely believe that now."

Marcel stayed in the bed with her until the morning. The next day, when the daylight shined through the windowpane, she was certain that Marcel was gone. Instead when her eyes focused, she saw his cell phone and wallet still on the dresser. A minute later she heard the juicer going in the kitchen again, and knew he was still home.

Marcel stayed in the house with her for five days, bathing her, changing her, feeding her and more than anything loving her. He told her everything she wanted to hear, and they talked about her hopes and dreams of being a successful writer, and his dreams of having enough money to take her to see the world. She was so full of joy that after awhile, she was physically better.

The morning she woke up feeling 100%, she was surprised when she felt warm lips against her pussy. Jewels opened her legs wider, and allowed him to do his business. His tongue ran up and down her clit, before he stiffened it and it dipped into her pussy tunnel.

"Oh, Marcel, oh Marcel, keep doing that shit," she encouraged.

It was the first orgasm that she experienced since she'd been ill, and she couldn't take it anymore. She allowed her cum to squirt all into his mouth, before she gripped both sides of his head.

It wasn't until she was satisfied, that she realized that the head she was holding between her hands, was smaller than usual. Quickly she snatched back the sheets to reveal Tree, one of the members of Marcel's gang.

"What are you doing here?" Jewels asked jumping out of bed, and taking the covers with her. "And where is Marcel?" she looked through the open door way, and saw no one.

"What's wrong, he said you were into chicks. I thought it was cool."

"Look, I'm not about this type of shit anymore, Tree," she placed her pants and shirt on. "I don't know what he told you but it's not me. Now where is my nigga?"

"Well Marcel had a job today, but he wanted me to be the one who made you feel good when you woke up," she responded.

Tree was a beautiful girl with gold and black hair, and bronzed skin. Jewels had met her a few times in passing, but they never experienced a moment like this. She felt violated, and just that quickly started to hate Marcel all over again.

"I appreciate the hook up and all, Tree, but I want to be alone right now."

"I guess so, you fucking came in my mouth already," she said putting on her clothes.

As she watched her leave the apartment, Jewels was starting to realize that she and Marcel were on two different paths when it came to their relationship. She also knew that unless he stepped up and treated her right, someone was going to get hurt and real soon.

CHAPTER 6

In The Courtroom:

As usual Jewels told the story how she wanted to tell it, but avoided the part about the girl, or getting her pussy licked. As far as the court would ever know, if she could help it, she was totally faithful to Marcel, and he had no reason to not trust her.

"So you're saying that the only time he showed affection was when you had the fever?" Adele asked her client.

"Yes, he took care of me until my fever was clear, but after that, he left me all alone. I didn't hear from him for three days," she said truthfully.

"Through all of this, you decided to marry him anyway, correct?"

She wiped her hair behind her ear, looked down into her lap and said, "Yes."

"But why, Juliette?"

"Because I thought things would change." She looked up from her hands and into her attorney's eyes. "And I wanted somebody to love me. I wanted him to make me feel good about myself."

Adele took two steps closer to the bench. "Did things change?"

"No"— she shook her head— "they didn't."

"Can you tell us about the day that he proposed?"

"Yes," she said wiping a tear from her eyes, "because it's a day I will never forget."

● ● ●

The Truth:
Summer, 2001

Jewels and Marcel was sitting in the back of the church in Boston, watching Crandon, one of Marcel's closest friends, get married. Jewels was consumed with jealousy, and the feeling was so strong, that she caused a bump of hate to form in the pit of her stomach. It was the fourth wedding that they'd been to together, and she didn't understand why this wasn't her life. She couldn't understand why Marcel wouldn't marry her, when she proved that despite how he treated her, she was still there.

As Jewels watched the bride walk down the aisle, she couldn't help but feel more jealousy brewing inside of her. Besides, Crandon met his wife after she met Marcel, and still she had not received a proposal. Why was Crandon's bride first?

Jewels looked at Marcel, who looked like money in his crisp black suit. "They look beautiful don't they," Jewels said softly to him. She leaned closer toward him and their shoulders touched. "You see how happy he looks. They're going to be so happy together."

"Don't start that shit, Jewels," he whispered heavily, looking straight ahead. "Because I ain't 'bout to be pressured into marrying you. I told you that shit already. I don't give a fuck who walking down the aisle."

She leaned away from him. "It's not about pressuring you, Marcel," she whispered. "It's about the fact that I love you, and you love me. It's about the fact that I have given you my everything and I feel like I'm not getting anything in return. You said you knew from the first moment you saw me that I was going to be your wife. If that's true, why don't I have your last name?"

"Juliette," he said harshly. He never said her real name unless he was thoroughly angry. "I'm sick of your fucking shit. I've given you everything you've ever wanted. I put a roof over your head, I clothed you and I keep you warm. What more do you want from me?"

"To be your fucking wife," she yelled, causing other people in the church to turn around. She stole the attention off of the bride, which was probably her unconscious hope.

"You know what, I'm sick of this shit," he yelled louder. "Since what I'm giving you now ain't good enough, I'm done trying. If you want a nigga to walk down the aisle with you, just leave me the fuck alone, and go find that dude. Because from here on out, I've decided that I'm done with you, and you can step the fuck off!"

While the two of them were arguing, Crandon's mother was on her way from the front of the church, to check them both. Both the bride and the groom stopped their vows just to see how things were going to play out.

"Let me make this clear, you two bastards got less than two seconds to get out of my baby's wedding, and if you don't..." The sound of weapons loading sounded off in the back of their heads. When they turned around, they saw Crandon's cousins who were not dressed for the occasion wearing jeans, and holding guns in their direction. "you won't make it out of this bitch alive. Leave now!"

Taking her at her word, both of them the left the small church. Dank moved to follow him but Marcel

said, "Go back in the church, man and support Crandon.
Tell him I'm sorry about this shit too."

When Dank reluctantly walked back inside, and they
made it outside, Marcel laid into her. "Do you see what
the fuck you just did? That was my man's wedding, Juliette." He pointed at the church. "I been knowing that
nigga for sixteen years! And you fucked it up off some
gay shit."

"I'm sorry, baby, I know it's just that I—"

"It ain't about you and what you want! It's about
what I want!"

She stepped back sensing his rage coming along.
"Marcel, I'm your girlfriend," she grabbed one of his
hands and looked into his eyes. "And I have done everything you've asked me to do. I have given you my virginity, I have slept with other women—"

"And you liked sleeping with other women too, so
don't put that shit on me," he snatched his hand away. "If
I recall you even came a few times."

"Yes, I did, Marcel. But I would have never gone
there if it weren't for you. And if I enjoyed myself a little
bit, and got my pussy ate, at the end of the day I earned
that right. But what I'm talking about is much bigger. I
wanna be your wife, Marcel. So if you won't ask me"—
she got on her knees – "then I'll ask you instead. Marcel
Madison, will you do me the honor of being my husband?"

Marcel looked down at her. He stepped closer and
was suddenly filled with blinding rage. Why this bitch
felt it was okay to pull this shit at his man's wedding was
beyond him. So on the steps of the church, he unzipped
his pants and pissed all over her face.

"Marcel," she yelled jumping up, wiping his urine from her eyes. "Why would you do that? In front of this church? That's so humiliating!"

"Fuck humiliation, bitch, you brought that on yourself," he zippered his pants. "I'm done with you, you hear me?" He walked off and towards the car. "And don't think about coming to the hotel, Jewels, because you won't be able to get in. Since you want to be a big girl, you on your own in Boston. See if you can find another nigga like me."

● ● ●

The Next Day

"You are so crazy, Garrick, I can't believe you remember that shit," Jewels said to him, as she sat on the bed in her motel room. Unlike before, this time she had three hundred dollars in her purse, and was able to get a room, and a bottle of wine to calm her nerves. "When I saw that roach in that lady's soup, who was sitting next to me at that shelter, and she ate it anyway, I fucking died."

He laughed harder. "She straight didn't give a fuck."

"Right, and had a nerve to ask for seconds," she sipped her wine.

"I guess some people just don't care," he chuckled harder, before gradually growing silent. "You hurt me, Juliette. You hurt me badly." Now it was time to talk about what was really going on, and the fact that she stood him up the last time.

"I know, Garrick and I'm so fucking sorry. I just...I mean...I didn't know how to walk away. I wanted so badly to do the right thing because I said that I would."

"Juliette, what's the real reason why you calling me now? 'Cause I need to be honest with you, I can't take the heartache anymore. So whatever you say to me, if you promise to be mine, only to take yourself away from me again, I'll never talk to you again. You understand what I'm saying? So don't tell me another thing you don't mean."

Jewels considered what he said and knew he was right. Garrick was the one man who had always been consistent in her life. There wasn't a thing in the world he wouldn't do for her, if she would only let him in. And luckily for him, after the way Marcel humiliated her on the steps of the church, she knew it was time to change.

"Garrick, I'm evil, I'm selfish and I'm mean at times." She lie face up on the bed and stared at the ceiling. "Sometimes I make decisions based on everybody else, and because of it, I act dumb. But I do know that I care about you. I really do, and I understand what you're saying, and I'm ready to make a decision and stand by it."

"So what is your decision?"

"I'm coming to LA to be with you," she said as her heart banged against the walls of her chest. "I'm so serious this time."

"Are you *really* serious, Juliette? Because I can't take another heartbreak from you." He paused. "And you need to know something else, I'm dating somebody." Her feelings were injured when she heard that, although he didn't belong to her. "But I'll throw her out in a minute to be with you, baby. You hear what I'm saying? So if you

71

truly love me, then you won't do me like this, because you're not only hurting me, you're hurting her too."

"Garrick, I know, I do care about you, and I'm ready. To commit, and if you knew what I went through you would understand, and believe me."

"If you're ready, I am too. So let me take care of your plane ticket, and I'll hit you back."

Juliette got off of the phone with him, and an hour later he called with her ticket information. "All you have to do is show your ID, and be on that flight in the a.m. I'll be waiting on you, baby."

"And I'll be there."

When she ended the call with him she called Marcel again. She knew it was wrong but she needed to do it for her own good. So that she could at least say she tried. And unlike the last five times she called; this time he answered the phone.

"Marcel, baby, I'm so glad you answered, because I have something very important to tell you."

He sighed. "Jewels, what is it?"

"Can you get a pen and a paper?"

"Look, I ain't got time for this shit," he yelled. "Anyway we over, so why you calling me?"

"Please, baby, just do what I'm asking."

When there was a pause, and she saw the line was not dropped, she figured he was honoring her request. So she waited for a minute and he returned with a pen and a paper.

"Now what?"

"At 8:00 in the morning, I will be on Flight 175 to LA."

He sighed. "Not this shit again, Jewels, I mean is this what you do? Threaten me with the existence of this other nigga, just so I can marry you? That shit old and if that's what you want and who you wanna be wit', then do you."

"That's not what I'm saying," she said softly, "what I'm saying is that I'll be there, in that airport, and that I still love you. If you want me as much as I want you, come for me, Marcel. Don't let me get on that plane. Because if you don't I'll be gone forever."

"Jewels, enjoy your life with old boy. I'm out."

The next morning, Jewels felt sick to her stomach. She knew that once she got on that plane, that the relationship as she knew it with Marcel would be over forever. When she replayed how he pissed on her in front of the church, and cheated on her relentlessly, she realized that Garrick would never do her that way and she deserved better. Maybe this was for the best. So she grabbed her things, hailed a cab and went to the airport.

Her body trembled like a volcano about to erupt, when she finally made it to Logan International Airport. She looked down, and could see her chest moving rapidly back and forth. *Are you sure about this Juliette?* She said to herself. *Did you just give up on the love of your life without a fight?* Even though Garrick was a good man, she didn't lust after him like she did Marcel. When she was around them her body reacted physically in different ways. Could she really see herself with Garrick for the rest of her life?

When she walked into the airport, and made it to the United Airlines counter, the woman asked for her name.

"I'm Juliette Jamison," she said softly, with a crooked smile.

"Ma'am, I can't hear you. Can you please speak up?"

Jewels cleared her throat and said, "I said that my name is Juliette Jamison."

The attendant keyed in a few items and said, "Ah yes, you have a business class seat on flight number 175." She smiled. "I'll check you in."

● ● ●

Marcel was on the toilet shitting his heart away, knowing that in a moment, the love of his life would be gone forever. Although the wedding was Sunday, he and Juliette had the room until Thursday. Before the fight, he planned to take her to some fine restaurants in Boston, before they headed back home, but her pushiness to get married ruined everything. And now she was gone.

He was so fucked up in the head that he didn't even go to the club, or bring another female to his room. Jewels was the first woman who loved him for him, and he let her get away for a nigga named Garrick.

After he flushed the toilet, he wiped his ass, washed his hands, and hopped back on the bed. When he turned the TV on, he was wondering why one of the World Trade Center towers in New York was smoking.

"What the fuck," he said turning the sound up on the television.

"*...yes, it appears that second FLIGHT 175 has crashed into the south tower of the World Trade Center,*" the newscaster reported.

A sharp pain that resembled a heart attack seized Marcel's chest. "Wait a minute. No! No! Please don't tell me..."

He leaped up and looked around the room for the paper where he'd written Juliette's flight information. When he remembered that he'd thrown it in the trashcan, he rushed toward it, knocking it over. After throwing several empty beer bottles on the floor, he finally located the piece of paper. When he opened it he saw clear as day FLIGHT 175 to LA.

"Oh my God, baby, I'm so fucking sorry! I'm so fucking sorry!"

In panic mode, Marcel rushed out of the hotel room, and approached a man who was getting into his car outside. Since his back was turned, he grabbed him by the shoulders and slammed his body into the side of the car, causing him to pass out. He then jumped into his ride and weaved in and out of traffic.

What a fucking fool he had been. She was the real deal and not only had he lost her, but he also lost her to death. He remembered the days he came into their bedroom, late at night, only to hear Jewels praying for his safety and sanity. Juliette's love for him was pure and unadulterated, and he didn't know what to do with it. He didn't know how to accept it, or handle it, because he was tormented inside. If she were on that plane, he would never be able to live with himself. He would probably go home, pull out the gun box, open it, load the weapon and put one hot slug into his head.

Once he made it to the airport, he was met with a frenzy of people. Some officers were yelling at other cars, and telling them that all flights were canceled. As a result, he was able to park the stolen car any kind of way, and rush inside. Everyone was glued to the screen on the TV, in which both of the towers were on fire. It felt like the world was on pause.

"Juliette," he yelled. "Juliette, please don't be on that plane."

When he happened upon a small group of people, and saw a woman a few feet in front of them pulling things out of her purse, and throwing them to the floor, his heart dropped. From the back her silhouette resembled his Juliette but he couldn't be sure. Slowly he approached her, afraid that his mind was playing tricks on him. Because if the information she gave him was correct at the motel, she should not be there. She should not be alive.

When he was close enough to her he took a deep breath and whispered, "Juliette..."

The woman turned around, stood up and wrapped her arms around him. "Oh my God, Marcel! I was supposed to be on that plane, baby! I was supposed to be on that plane, but I can't find my ID!"

"I know, I know, baby," he choked up and tried to force back his tears. He wiped her face backwards with both hands and looked into her eyes. "Jewels, I love you so much, and I'm a fucking fool. Sometimes I play the dumb nigga but this shit today made me realize what you mean to me. I'll never lose you again, and I'll never let you go. You belong to me, and I don't care who I have to kill or hurt to protect what's mine. You gotta let that nigga Garrick know, baby. You gotta tell him you belong to me, because I can't go through this shit again."

"I will, baby," she trembled. "I will."

He backed away from her and got on one knee. In the middle of the airport, surrounded by turmoil and dismay, he grabbed her hand, looked up at her and said, "Juliette Jamison, I love you more than anything in this entire world. I know I'm a fool, but your patience with me is one of the reasons why I can't lose you. You are God sent, Jewels. I guess what I'm asking you is, will you do me the honor of being my wife?"

Tears fell down her face and onto his. "Yes, baby, yes!"

CHAPTER 7

In The Courtroom:

As Jewels sat on the stand, she was praying that she did a good job with her testimony. Even when she recalled Marcel proposing to her, she never spoke about Garrick, or his undying love for her. She left out the part of her being in the airport to meet another man, and told the court that she was trying to get away to clear her mind, by going to LA.

After the defense attorney finished with Jewels, the prosecutor requested to re-question her before she left the stand. Although uncommon, the judge allowed it.

"So you claim that Marcel was selfish, that he urinated on you in public, and was almost the cause of you dying on an airplane."

"That's correct."

"But, isn't it also true that Marcel was not just a provider, like you explained when he put you up in the apartment, but also very generous?"

Jewels wiped her hair backwards with her hand, and tried to think of where the prosecutor was going. When she realized she had no idea she asked, "What do you mean?"

"Well we all can agree that based on your earlier testimony, that even if Marcel left the taco truck, and was later employed as a manager at a fast food chain, he didn't have access to a lot of money. Wouldn't you say that's correct?"

She looked at her attorney and couldn't read her expression. Did Adele want her to be honest or not? She had to wing it. "I mean, he had some money, but not a lot."

"Perfect! Then the fact that he spent a thousand dollars on your engagement ring, says a lot about his character doesn't it?"

"It depends on how you look at it I guess. But, Marcel always did what he wanted to do, and most of the time it had nothing to do with me. After awhile, Marcel didn't want to do nothing for me. Even the ring he bought me for our wedding was a fake. He got it from some cheap department store. I think it was FloorMart," she said, trying to keep a straight face. "He damn sure didn't spend no thousand dollars like he told me."

The Truth:
Winter, 2001

"Baby, listen to this song," Marcel said as he turned his radio up, inside of his new black Rolls-Royce Bentley. "Nas murdered this shit."

As Juliette looked over at him, her heart fluttered. It seemed like everything he did looked good. Like the way the running heat teased the hairs on his chocolate fur coat, while the diamond ring in his ear hit the sunlight and sparkled. Since Marcel had expanded his business to include drugs, he made a huge come up, and stayed looking like a bag of money.

Jewels sat in the passenger seat and waited for the song that had her fiancé so excited. Something was on her mind, but she was controlling it, for fear that she would lose him again with her pushiness. Although he hadn't bothered to get her an engagement ring yet, the fact that he proposed gave her hope that one-day he would actually marry her. However, as the days went by, she was starting to believe that it wasn't the case.

Marcel bopped is head as Jewels listened to the radio, in which Nas ripped into Jay Z's asshole with his latest song, *Ether*. She couldn't believe he was going so hard at Jay Z, especially since as far as she knew they were friends.

'How much of Biggie's rhymes is goin' come out your fat lips? Wanted to be on every last one of my classics. You pop shit, apologize, nigga, just ask Kiss...'

"Babe, can you believe Nas ate into him like that?" Marcel said turning down the radio when the song was over. "There's no way in the world Jay gonna be able to come back after that. And that's my man!"

"Naw, I can't believe it," she said dryly, looking out of the window.

What I want to know is when the fuck are you gonna make me your wife, and give me my ring? Fuck a song!

Jewels' beautiful long hair was whipped over her shoulder, as she crossed her arms and looked out of the passenger window.

Marcel looked over at her, sensing her irritation. "What's wrong with my wifey?" He asked, as he continued to steer the car down the road. Ever since 9/11 he appreciated her more, although sometimes she acted like a spoiled brat. But lately Marcel was careful about how he went at her, figuring he would lose her forever. "Talk to me, Jewels."

Since he wanted to talk she decided to cut into him like a butcher knife. "For starters you keep calling me your wifey when I'm not. I think just saying the shit has made you comfortable and I'm not with it."

Marcel laughed and shook his head. "You know what, I love when you get mad at me. There's something about the way your lips poke out, and the way you roll your eyes, that just gets my dick hard."

"I'm so happy I can do that for you," she said rolling her eyes, while wiggling her foot quickly.

Marcel decided to leave her alone, and he eventually pulled up in front of a beautiful building in Georgetown, DC. He eased out of the car, and walked toward the passenger side.

When he opened the door for her, for a moment Jewels took in his honey brown skin, and his golden hair, and tried not to allow her pussy to get wet. She caught the girl who was at the light, in the car next to theirs, staring at him. The bitch was Hollywooding so hard she almost crashed her car.

Marcel said, "Come on, baby. We gotta make a stop right quick."

Jewels stepped out, and pulled her white mink closer together, to battle the December chill. She placed her red Christian Louboutin onto the curb, with the help of Marcel's hand, as he opened the door for her to the building. The moment they stepped inside of the establishment, a white woman greeted them, while holding a tray containing two glasses of sparkling champagne.

"Good evening, Mr. Madison and Ms. Jamison," she handed Jewels a flute and then Marcel. "We've been waiting on you."

Once they were inside an armed security guard locked the door behind them. "Baby, what's going on?"

Jewels asked, taken aback by the world-class treatment. "Why does that lady know my name? And why did the security guard just lock the door?"

"You'll see in a moment," he winked, as he walked her across the marble floor, and toward the counter. When she looked down, her breath was stolen by all of the diamond ice that blinged from every direction. She was completely captivated.

The moment she approached the counter, a beautiful black woman had three velvet black trays displayed before her, with the most beautiful diamond rings that she'd ever seen in her life sitting upon them.

Marcel sat his champagne glass down and looked at his fiancé. "Jewels, I know I always fuck up, but nothing's more important to me than making your wedding day special. Now I could've come here, and made a decision without you, but I don't wanna do that no more. You my world, baby, and its important that we make decisions together." A tear fell down her eyes and he wiped it away with his thumb. "What you crying for, beautiful?"

"I'm so...I'm so, happy," she said trying not to explode from joy.

"Well we not even done yet. So, I want you to choose any diamond ring you want, with the understanding that there is no price tag too big for you."

Jewels was shivering. "Marcel"- she eyed the rings- "are you serious?"

"I'm diamond serious," he winked. "Now choose."

Jewels spent and hour going over clarity and carat size with the knowledgeable sales rep. When she was done she selected a five-carat diamond ring. "This is the one, baby," she said jumping up and down, while holding it firmly in her hand. "This is the one I want!"

He looked at the sales representative and said, "You heard my, baby, this one is it. Ring it up!"

He got on his knees, took the ring, grabbed her hand and looked into her eyes. "Jewels, I asked you to be my wife on September 11th, but I was distressed. I'm not right now and I know who I want by my side. So, Juliette Jamison, would you do me the honor of changing your last name?"

"Yes, baby," she said kissing him when he stood up. "You know I will."

Luckily for Jewels the ring fit perfectly, so after they cleaned it, she walked out of the store on cloud nine with it blinging on her hand. She was so busy gawking at the ring that she didn't realize that they were going nowhere near the house, until thirty minutes later.

"Baby, where are we?" she looked around the luxurious neighborhood. "We can't be anywhere near our apartment."

Marcel parked the car in front of a million dollar red brick home. The yard was covered with snow blanketed large oak trees, and a water fountain sat in the driveway. Marcel opened the door for her again, and helped her out of the car.

"Baby, what is this?" she asked looking up at the spectacular home. "Who lives here?"

All he did was wink, and walked her into the house. When he opened the door, even though the home was empty, Jewels' breath was again taken away. The large foyer, the crystal chandeliers, the marble floor, the chocolate banister, everything was like a scene from the rich and famous or in a movie. Marcel snapped his fingers, and a second later, two white women walked out of the back with huge smiles on their faces, and big catalogs clutched in their hands.

"Baby, this is the new home I bought for us."
Jewels fainted.

When she woke up, and he made sure she was okay, he explained everything to her in slow motion so that she could handle it. Feeling better already, she spent the next five minutes jumping up and down, doing the Cabbage Patch and slobbing Marcel down in front of the women. He understood that since she started fucking with him she went from a shelter to a million dollar home in less than two years. So he allowed her to do her thing.

"Baby, this is our new home," he repeated, while grinning. "And these are your interior decorators. They have some books for you to look over. You pick whatever furniture you desire, along with the color schemes, and they'll fix it up for us in a week."

"What about the apartment? And our things? I have to pack! There's so much to do, Marcel."

"It's all been taken care of," he said. "Now hurry up and make your selections. I have one other place to take you."

Musha Cay
The Islands of Copperfield Bay

Marcel spared no expense on Jewels. He wanted to make sure that she realized that Garrick, or nobody else, could provide her with the lifestyle he could. He wanted her so spoiled that after he got through with her, she would be upgraded and expect nothing less from any other dude she fucked with.

While their new home was being decorated, he whisked her away to Musha Cay, the private Island that the magician David Copperfield built. The trip alone was $60,000 and it was worth the money. The property sat on 150 acres of sparkling white sugar beaches, with crystal blue water and beautiful exotic flowers everywhere. It was exactly how Jewels envisioned Heaven would be.

After they skinny-dipped, made love and grabbed something to eat, they took a nap in their master suite that overlooked the beach. They were lying in bed, looking at the view when Juliette said, "Marcel, I can't believe you did all of this for me." She looked at the scenery again, trying to burn it into her mind forever.

"Believe it, baby," he said rubbing her hair. "You fucking with a real nigga now, and there's no going back."

"What did I do to deserve you?"

"Besides almost dying on an airplane, and making me realize where I would be if I didn't have you in my life?" he joked.

"Yes," she smiled.

"Outside of that, all you did was love me...unconditionally. You weren't like them other bitches, who wanted me but didn't want to adapt to who I was. You love and love hard, so I have to make you my wife."

"What can I do to keep this moment forever?" she sat up in bed and looked at him.

"Never change," he said plainly.

"Of course I won't change, Marcel."

"I'm serious, Jewels. I'm the kind of nigga who loves excitement, and variety. The reason I'm making you my wife is because you never changed me. And I realized when I almost lost you, how hard it would be to find someone like you." he sat up and rubbed her shoulders. "You're beautiful, got a body I'd kill for and I was the first one whoever tapped that pussy. You was wifey material for sure, so it's only right that I queen you."

"This is all so deep."

"I know, but it's true," he said kissing her. "Look at where we are, Jewels. You helped me build this. If it weren't for you keeping me on my toes, and keeping me grounded, we wouldn't be in a place like this. But more than anything you allowed me to be me." He paused. "You feel what I'm really saying?"

"Of course, Marcel."

"That's good, baby, because even though you my wife, I need you to always be you, and I need for you to allow me to be me. That's our secret. That's how we stay together and make our marriage last."

CHAPTER 8

In The Courtroom:

"So you say that he gave you an engagement ring, and presented it to you at his job," the prosecutor asked, after listening to Jewels' shaky testimony. "So in doing so, you will admit that he was more generous than you let on earlier. And that you are a liar who is doing nothing more than trying to win sympathy from the jury."

"I object, prosecution is badgering the witness," Adele yelled, standing up.

"Objection sustained," the judge responded.

"I'll rephrase the question," the prosecutor said. "Do you believe that Marcel showed how much he loved you, buy purchasing a ring he couldn't afford?"

"At one time he loved me, but it had nothing to do with the ring, plus like I said I think it was fake. He just did things for show."

"What do you mean?"

"I believe that he loved what having a wife represented, but I'm not sure that he ever loved me, or really pictured himself with me for the long haul. Plus the wedding was a disaster."

"Please elaborate."

The Truth:

Some months after Musha Cay they decided to tie the knot, they were discussing their future. The night before their wedding Marcel and Jewels were standing in the kitchen, going over last minute details.

"Baby, this wedding won't be like anybody's wedding we've ever been to before," Marcel said. "This shit is going to be all the way live. I'm talking epic."

She sighed because when she envisioned getting married, she certainly didn't see the large party he planned. "What do you mean?"

"Well after the wedding, the gang is planning a major party for me."

"Shouldn't they have done that last night? At your bachelor party?"

"But we having another party too," he said over excitedly which made Jewels' ass itch. "Now I know you're use to those stuffy wedding receptions that we go to all the time." He poured her a glass of red wine, and grabbed a beer out of the refrigerator for himself. "But ours is going down in history as the wedding to remember. Crandon and his new wife are going to be sick when they see how fly our reception is. It's gonna be way better than theirs. We hired strippers, a Go-Go band and some professional singers. We all the way live, baby."

"Marcel, I kind of wanted to chill with you," she said walking up to him, rubbing his shoulders softly. "I mean, this day is about us not the party right?"

"And you will be with me," he kissed her forehead. "You not gonna be having all of the fun alone." He chuckled. "This is just a view of how our life together will be."

This scared the shit out of her. She wanted him to calm down not kick it up another notch after they got married. "I'm talking about without everybody else," Jewels said. "I don't need no party and shit. All I need is you."

Marcel frowned and stepped away from her. "Jewels, what are you talking about? I took you to Musha Cay, and bought you that five-carat engagement ring on your finger. Not to mention the fact that I put you up in this beautiful home. The least you can do is give a nigga a break, and let me bring in our new life right. The way that I want to. I feel like you got everything and I got shit."

"Marcel, this isn't fair. A wedding is about the bride and groom, not stunts and shows." She paused. "I mean, you do realize that you're about to be a married man don't you? You have to understand that, all of the things we use to do in our relationship can't go down anymore."

"Why, Jewels," he yelled slamming the beer on the counter. "Why should the excitement be stopped?"

"Not the excitement between us. I'm talking about the excitement with other people. When you're my husband, outside of the weekends, I'm going to want you alone, Marcel. I'm going to want to start a quiet life with you, so that we can raise a family. I mean, if you wanted to still sleep with other women, and lead a life of a bachelor, why marry me?"

"Because I love you, Jewels, I truly do, but I can't be put into a box no more. I won't." When he saw the disappointment in her eyes he walked over to her. "Remember when we were in Musha Cay, and you told me you would never change me. This is what I'm talking about right here."

"Marcel, this isn't fair."

"It is fair, baby. I'm gonna always hang out with my friends, and I'm gonna always do me. Are you saying you can't get wit' that?"

"I'm saying I want you, Marcel," she looked at the engagement ring on her finger. "And I'm saying that I don't wanna share you anymore. Think about how you would feel if my attention was elsewhere. Wouldn't that hurt you?"

He laughed. "Jewels, look at you." He snatched her by the arm, and took her to the bathroom on the basement level so she could see herself in the mirror. "You go to a luxury salon every week," he pulled a few strands of her beautiful black mane. "You get your makeup done professionally at least three times a month just because. And, you have rows and rows of designer handbags in your arsenal. Look at you. You are a made woman because you fuck with me. Now picture another nigga being able to compete with that. So, do you want to give it all up, just because I like to have a little fun?"

"I'm saying I want you alone, and that I can't deal with the life we led before."

"Then I guess we ain't getting married then," he said, walking out and leaving her in the bathroom alone.

The next morning, on her wedding day, she woke up to see Marcel was still not home. Hurt, she took a shower and cried her eyes out. Her wedding day began with a break up instead of the path leading to a new future. Once again, her plight to keep Marcel all to herself ended in not having him at all. She waited so long to get to this moment, and now it wasn't hers anymore. She wondered would he even be at the small church, where their wedding ceremony would be taken place, or was he done with her all together.

Reluctantly she got dressed anyway, and slid into her wedding dress. It was at that moment that it dawned on her that she didn't have a life outside of Marcel. Her friends were his. Her life was his. There was no identity outside of her life with him. Her wedding validated this point. All of her bridesmaids, even Gia, her maid of honor, who she hated with a passion, were all in her life as a result of Marcel. She was beyond depressed and she could hear her mother's voice telling her not to marry him. Juliette knew their relationship was wrong, which is also why she never told him of her past life in Honduras. The saddest part is, he never bothered to ask either.

After she was dressed, she walked outside. The white limousine she rented was there, and a beautiful female driver with chocolate skin, and gold and black hair opened the door to let her inside. She looked more like a model than anything else.

Once they both were back inside of the limo the driver said, "My name is Bet, can I take you to the church? Or did you want to stop somewhere else first?"

Jewels stared ahead of her. "Yes, please. The church is fine."

"No problem," she responded.

As they drove to the church in silence Jewels wondered would he show up. Fifteen minutes later when she got there, she received her answer as she walked into the small chapel. Not only was the church empty, because all of her friends were his friends, but not even the minister was present.

When she stepped out of the place of worship still as Jewels Jamison instead of Jewels Madison, Bet was standing there waiting. "That nigga didn't show up did he?" Bet asked. "What a bum." When Jewels started crying she felt bad. "I'm sorry, I didn't mean to come at you like that."

"It doesn't even matter, because it's true."

There was something about her honesty, despite not knowing her, that made Jewels immediately like her. She was just the driver, yet the words she chose to use made Jewels feel like she wasn't alone in the moment.

Jewels walked to the limousine. "Can you just take me home please? I can't take this right now."

"Sure," she said.

When they were back inside of the limo, instead of hearing her own voice Jewels asked Bet to turn the radio on. The moment she did she heard Ashanti's new song *Foolish*.

"See my days are cold without you, but I'm hurting while I'm with you. And though my heart can't take no more I keep on running back to you..."

That's how she felt. Like an idiot. After all, who else would allow someone to treat them so badly, and still stand in their corner? Tears continued to pour from her eyes until her cell phone rang in her lap.

When she answered she heard his voice. "Do you know what it feels like to lose me yet? Or do I have to punish you even more?"

An immediate sense of relief overcame her. It was similar to what she felt when she lost her purse at the mall, but found out that a nice sales rep. put it behind the counter, until she returned.

"Yes, baby, I do! Please come back to me, Marcel. Don't do me like this. I mean we came so far."

He chuckled, and in a sly tone said, "Yeah, it sounds like you learned your lesson." His arrogance made her stomach rumble. "But look, come to the place where the party is. I'm waiting on you there."

The next question she needed to know but was afraid to ask, before she went any further. "Are we still getting married, Marcel?"

"Not if you don't hurry up before the Reverend, who is here with me, gets too drunk."

At Martins Crosswinds

When Bet pulled the limo up to Martins Crosswinds, she rolled the privacy window down to look back at Jewels. "We're here, did you want me to walk you inside?"

Jewels looked up at her and said, "Please...because I'm so confused right now on what Marcel is doing. I would appreciate your support." She wanted someone to be there in her corner, and Bet stepped up to do the job. She definitely was going to give her a major tip behind all of this.

First Bet opened Jewels' door and helped her out. Bet held Jewels' train, and walked her into the ballroom. The moment they walked inside, she was shocked when she saw the party was in full mode. The entire wedding party was there and the groomsmen were dressed up in tuxedos with their ties open. It was as if the wedding already occurred without her.

"Where is your fiancé?" Bet asked, looking around.

"I don't know." She shrugged. "He told me to meet him, so he has to be here somewhere."

The moment she said that, Marcel appeared with an open bottle of Moet in his hand. His tuxedo was still on, but it was totally unraveled. She could tell by the redness of his eyes that he was drunk, and this angered her even more. All he wanted was a party, not a wedding and she contemplated punching him in the face.

The moment he saw her he said, "Now there's my fucking wife." He rushed up to her and slobbed her down, and she was disgusted by the stanky taste of his breath. "Now the party can officially begin."

When she looked into the ballroom, she saw strippers all over the tables, flashing their coochies. "Marcel, are we getting married?" she looked around the room. "Because it looks like you're married already if you ask me."

He frowned. "Baby, stop the dumb shit, damn. You here because you accept that I'm going to do me, and you know you can't live without me. So just come with me and lets do this shit," he said grabbing her by the hand.

Bet followed them both and Marcel walked up to Reverend Morgan, who was at the table, drinking wine with two women who were scantly dressed, and sitting on his lap. "Morgan, Jewels is here, and we ready, man."

The moment the Reverend smiled at her, Jewels could tell that he was also inebriated. "Juliette, you were already beautiful the last time I saw you, but now you're even more stunning," he stood up and almost fell back down. Eventually he was standing on his own two feet, after Marcel shoved him. He grabbed the black bible off of the table and said, "Do you Marcel Madison, take—"

"Wait," she said looking at Marcel. "We doing this in here?"

"Yeah," Marcel said looking into her eyes. "Don't you wanna be my wife?"

"Of course, baby," she looked around, and then at Bet who looked away due to the embarrassment. "But I don't wanna do it like this. Can't we go somewhere more private at least? In another room? I wrote down some things I wanted to say to you in my vows, at the alter. I can't say them here."

"Jewels, I love you, you love me. What difference does it make if we get married here or in a church? Let's not waste any more time with this shit or your corny ass vows, because I'm getting irritated again." he focused on the Reverend. "Finish, man, so I can marry this bitch right quick."

Jewels was totally humiliated.

"Not a problem," the Reverend cleared his throat. "Do you, Marcel Madison, take Juliette Jamison to be your lawfully wedded wife?"

"I do," Marcel smiled widely, before taking a swig of Moet.

"And do you, Juliette Jamison, take Marcel Madison..."

After this point she blanked out. Although she remembered saying I do, she didn't remember saying much else. She couldn't believe that the day she dreamed about, ever since he first proposed, was going down in such a ratchet way. Go-Go music played loudly in the background, while strippers danced on the table, and Marcel's crew made it rain on them. And there she and Marcel stood, in the midst of the mess, getting married for the rest of their lives. She was beginning to hate him even more.

At the end of the party, which Jewels eventually got so drunk that she almost passed out, her and Marcel climbed back into the limo. Marcel was all paws at this point, and he groped his wife like a cheap whore, without caring about her feelings or mood.

When the limo finally stopped, they were at the Four Seasons hotel in Baltimore. Marcel purchased the Executive Suite, for their wedding. After they checked in and walked into the suite, the moment they got inside Jewels was disgusted at what she saw. In the bed, was Gia, and two other women who were naked.

Excited, Marcel jumped into the bed and was immediately surrounded by the women as they wrapped their legs around him.

"Happy wedding day, BFF," Gia said, whipping her long hair out of her face as she straddled Jewels' new husband, without a stitch of clothing on her body. "I flew two of my Italian friends all the way from Italy to share this special day with you." She kissed him passionately and then looked back at Jewels. "Come on, Jewels," she said slyly. "One of them is here for you too."

Jewels walked out of the suite, and slept in Bet's Limousine.

CHAPTER 9

In The Courtroom:

"You have to understand that after Marcel spent the money for the ring, the wedding at the small chapel, and the party at the community center, he was dead broke. He didn't have a lot of money and he tried to blame me just because I wanted a wedding."

Once again Jewels remixed the story. Although she told the truth about being left at the alter, and getting married at the reception party, she told the court that the reception was held in the community center. She was a master at taking the suspicion off of her. In fact, she didn't tell them where they were even living at this point. As far as the court knew, she still lived in an apartment, and not in a million dollar home.

"What do you mean blame you?" the prosecutor asked.

"He always felt like he needed to do more for me, even though I assured him that I was okay with our normal lifestyle."

"Did he feel like that because you made him feel that way?"

"Of course not," she refuted, "I always made Marcel feel that all I wanted was him, because it was the truth. I let him know daily that I was comfortable where we were living, and with the money we had. At the end of the day, all I wanted was his love."

The Truth:
Spring, 2002

Jewels was sitting on the couch in her living room, with a bunch of balled up used tissue thrown on the couch, and on the floor in front of her. She was crying her eyes out, because one of her favorite singers, *Left Eye* from the group TLC, was killed in Honduras, Jewels' hometown. When she learned that it was during a car accident, she was even more distraught.

She was supposed to be talking to Bet on the phone, but she couldn't get herself together. After the wedding about a month ago, she and Bet became very close friends. Bet became the rock she needed in her life, when Marcel was cold and selfish, like he had been lately. In Marcel's mind, Jewels should be honored that he chose to make her Mrs. Madison in the first place, and he carried himself accordingly. Being a faithful husband was the last thing on his mind.

Everyday it was work for Jewels not to hold a special place of hate in her heart for her husband, and she was tired of it. Tired of having to remind herself every morning that there was a reason she married him, even though she couldn't see why.

"Bet, I still can't believe *Left Eye* is dead," Jewels cried harder. "Do you realize how much I loved their music? Their songs got me through life when I first got with Marcel."

"I know it's sad, Jewels, and I understand you're upset. A lot of people are shocked by the news, but are you sure that you aren't crying about something else?"

"What do you mean," Jewels said, snatching a fresh tissue paper from the box, to wipe her wet eyes.

"How do you know that you aren't really crying because after all this time, you still don't have a solid relationship with your husband?"

"I know Marcel ain't about shit, but I love him, and he loves me. I know he's going to change, it just hasn't happened yet."

"Jewels, haven't you heard the saying that if somebody tells you who they are, that you should believe them?"

"No, Bet," she sighed.

"You expected him to not be who he was when you got with him. I mean I know we are fast friends, but I feel like I've known you all of my life and I have to keep shit real with you. Maybe you were hoping that after he made you his wife, he would give all of the partying up. When he told you to your face what he was about."

"I don't know, Bet, I mean, he does seem meaner now. I guess I just feel like its something I'm doing. When he comes home, if I don't want to participate in some crazy orgy he has planned, or go to some wild party, he doesn't want to spend time with me at all."

"Have you ever thought about getting your marriage annulled?"

"Annulled?" Jewels frowned. "I will never leave my husband, Bet! Ever! You have to understand; before Marcel came into my life I was alone. I didn't have anything or anyone, and I will not abandon him, because he didn't abandon me. What I'm going to do is give him the next six months to get this crazy shit out of his system."

"Jewels, that nigga is never changing. Listen to your-self, look at your husband and follow his actions. What you see with Marcel is what you're going to get!"

"I think you need to check yourself, Bet, I fuck with you and all but you did just meet me."

"I hear all that but I'm going to say it again, that nig-ga ain't never changing," she continued, never afraid to speak her mind. "And you need to be clear on something when dealing with me too. I never bite my tongue, Jew-els, ever."

"It's not about you biting your tongue, it's just...Bet...I mean...I'm so confused right now." She dropped her head. "All I wanted him to do was love me."

"I know, Jewels, and I don't mean to come down hard on you, but I'm your friend, not his. Marcel is going to take as much advantage of you as you allow him. If I were you, I'd be stashing money to the side, and prepar-ing to get your life together without him, in the event you have to step off and leave his ass alone."

Bet was talking some real shit but it was too much for Jewels to decipher. "Alright, Bet," she said. "I gotta go. I'll talk to you later."

Jewels wasn't ready to receive her words of wisdom. All she knew was that she loved Marcel, and that he was the only person who ever stood in her corner, not exclud-ing Garrick. Marcel was the first person who told her how to move her body when they were making love. He was the first person who showed her the luxury life, and she didn't want to give up on him so soon.

While she was in her mind, Marcel came through the front door enraged and covered in blood.

"Fuck," he yelled knocking a fifteen thousand dollar vase on the floor, causing it to shatter into a million piec-es.

Instead of stopping there, he went through the house like a cyclone, spinning around and breaking everything not nailed to the wall. Afraid but bold, Jewels walked up to him before he did more damage and said, "Marcel, what's wrong?"

"Dank, was murdered, man! I fucking told him to watch his back, Jewels but the nigga didn't listen to me. These bammas at the dealership yanked him, pressed the barrel to his face and... pulled the trigger, baby. FUCK!" he screamed fighting at the air. "My nigga was massacred!"

She tried to hold him but he pushed her away. "What the fuck am I going to do with my man gone? Huh? This nigga had my back when nobody else did!"

She felt selfish for wanting herself to be the person to hold him down, instead of Dank. But it was like she was invisible to him. "I'm so sorry, baby," she said keeping her distance. "Maybe I can make you a drink."

"That ain't helping me with shit, Jewels," he said angrily. "You always saying the wrong things. I need Gia on the phone."

What a low blow. There she was, willing and able to support him, and he wanted Gia.

"And then the cops had the nerve to lock up Courtney," he continued, "because she didn't want to leave his body out there on the pavement. I feel like laying into somebody right now, Jewels. Be very careful on how you talk to me tonight." He stepped up to her like he was going to kill her. "And I suggest you stay the fuck away from me too."

There he goes making me eat his shit again. She thought.

"Marcel, I'm not the enemy. I'm the one who loves you remember?"

"You don't love me," he snatched her wedding finger, and almost pulled it out of the socket. "You just love what I can do for you, and what I can provide." He dropped her hand. "It's because of all of the shit you want, that I lost my man. This is part your fault."

She backed up feeling a beating coming on. "Marcel, that is so fucking not fair."

"Why is that not fair," he looked up at the vaulted ceiling. "Look at this house." He raised his arms to his sides. "Look at your BMW out front, Jewels. My money made you, and you have no idea what I have to go through to get it. Think about this shit right here when you want to pressure me about not coming home and dumb shit like that!"

"Marcel, I'm with you because I love you, not for the money or what you can do for me."

"You really believe that shit don't you?" he walked into the kitchen, and grabbed a bottle of vodka out of the freezer. A fog of cold air rolled out before disappearing.

"Have you forgotten that I'm the one who stayed with you when you were living with your mother?"

"We stayed with my mother for one day, Jewels," he reminded her. He turned the top and poured the liquor down his throat.

"But you stayed there every night in the beginning, and you put me up in a hotel. But I still remained with you until we got our apartment."

"Yeah, but you always saw the potential didn't you? Tell the truth, Jewels, you knew that at some point if you hung in there with me, that you would come out on the good end of this shit. And guess what, you did."

"Marcel, I would give this shit up in a heartbeat if it meant keeping our marriage strong. As a matter of fact, let's do it. Let's take the money we have," she stepped closer to him, "sell this house and start all over again. I'm willing to give all of this illegal shit up if you are."

"You sound stupid," he said gritting on her. "I will never be broke, not for you, or nobody else, bitch." He drank more vodka, and stomped away.

Once he was in the library, he slammed the door behind him. Jewels cleaned the mess he caused, and she didn't see him for two hours. When he walked back into the living room, he seemed revived. It was as if he was a totally different person.

"I found the answer," he said walking up to her.

He had showered and was in a different mood. Jewels was in the living room drinking wine and listening to old TLC cd's.

"And what's that?" she said rolling her eyes. For all she cared at the moment, he could go shoot himself in the nostrils.

"I know you not still mad at me for earlier, Jewels. I'm sorry I snapped at you, but I had a lot on my mind. You need to thank Gia because she was able to hook me up with someone who worked in the mafia at one point. He not all the way in though so I gotta convince him that he can trust me. Baby, he sick with breaking locks, cracking alarm codes and some more shit. If I can get him to know I'm good peoples, this could be the break my squad was looking for. We in there, wifey. Go comb your hair, and shit you look crazy."

Fuck you, nigga. She thought. She didn't comb shit.

Jewels couldn't speak on other bitches, but personally she hated the wifey tag. In her opinion it was just a way for a nigga to have a main bitch, but not fully commit.

When the doorbell rang, Marcel walked away to go answer it. He was as happy as a faggy in a room full of male strippers. Suddenly Jewels was enamored about who had her husband bright eyed. She had to meet this mysterious man.

The moment Marcel opened the front door, and she saw the man's face, her heart stopped. The mystery man was Spanish and black, and his long hair was pulled back into a ponytail. His body was muscular, but not too big and tats were everywhere on his arms. He resembled the wrestler turned actor, *The Rock*, in his younger years.

"What's up, man," Marcel said dapping the stranger, before pulling him into a manly hug. "I heard a lot about you from Gia. Welcome to my home."

"I heard a lot about you too," he said, trying not to look at the woman behind him, who had taken his breath away. "I just hope I can"— he looked at Jewels— "be a contribution"— he looked at Jewels again— "to your squad."

"Damn, Gia told me I had to work a little harder to convince you to roll with me. Come on in, man, we have a lot to discuss." he walked him up to Jewels. "Oh, before I forget, this is my wifey, Jewels." He shook her hand and held onto it tightly. "And Jewels, this is Wade Wallace, the nigga I was just telling you about."

Her stomach swirled and her heart raced. Up until that point she believed that Marcel was the true love of her life. But one thing was for certain, and it was that after she met Wade Wallace, she would never be the same.

CHAPTER 10

In The Courtroom:

"You talk a lot about how bad he was to you, but isn't it true that you also were unfaithful, and slept around?" the prosecutor asked.

"Never, I was never unfaithful to my husband," she responded looking directly into his eyes. "I told you that before, and I don't know why you keep asking me."

Throughout her testimony, she was careful about not letting on about anything she did, so she wasn't worried by what he said.

"Are you sure, because we have witness testimony that you have slept around during your marriage," the prosecutor continued.

"I don't care what you have, I never slept around on my husband before," Jewels said, slightly raising her voice. "I loved him!"

When she focused back on her attorney, the look Adele gave caused her to calm down a little. Adele didn't want her losing her composure, which she was sure was the prosecutor's aim.

"Like I said, I was never unfaithful to my husband, but he was unfaithful to me," she said leaning in. "I was the best wife I could be, and I worked overtime to make our marriage new and fresh. He was the one who kept violating our bond and if you don't believe me, there's nothing more I can say about it."

The Truth:
Summer, 2002

Marcel, Jewels, Wade and the gang were front row at the Pyramid Arena, watching Mike Tyson and Lennox Lewis battle it out. It was the fifth round and Mike wasn't shining at all, even though most hoped that he could make a comeback. Outside of everybody in the arena, there was no one more loud and ridiculous than Marcel.

Not only was he yelling obscenities, and scaring the hell out of his wife, he had Gia to his right, and another woman to his left, while Jewels sat a few seats over.

However, sitting on the other side of Jewels was Wade, and he was driving her crazy with his sex appeal. It was as if she was a vampire and she wanted to taste his blood. She wanted him away from her...now!

Although she was avoiding him, Marcel made a smart move by bringing him to the team. Both his drug and robbery businesses had tripled its profits since Wade was on security. Marcel had hit ten dealerships in the Texas area, and five in Virginia, which all netted him half of million dollars. With that he bought some cocaine bricks at a good rate, which he was able to distribute due to his connections. He felt invincible and on top of the world.

"What the fuck is Mike Tyson doing," Marcel yelled again. "I got fifty grand on this nigga," he said to Gia, and whoever else was listening to his boasting.

"I don't know about all that," Gia said seductively, "It looks like you're going to be out of fifty if you ask me." She winked. "But me, well I'm very smart because I put my money on Lennox."

"You may be beautiful but you still dumb," Marcel told her, patting her on the head like a kid.

Jewels, frustrated with not getting the attention from her husband, sighed loudly and dropped her head. With the pat on the head Gia had already got more attention than she did. She was doing all she could to get him to notice her but nothing worked. She even wore a beautiful orange summer dress that showcased her cleavage and round hips. But it was all in vain, because hubby could care less.

When Wade saw Jewels' frustration, he placed a soft hand over hers, causing chills to run through her body. She was trying her best to avoid him, but it was something about Wade that called her name.

When she knew he was coming over to her house, she would find a reason to be gone. When Marcel was having a meeting with the gang, she would purposely be nowhere in sight. And finally when they were supposed to be hanging out at a club, and she got word that Wade would be present, she would not show up. The only reason that they were in each other's presence at the fight was because one of the other gang members couldn't go, and Wade bought the ticket. In the back of her mind, she wondered if it was because of her.

"How you doing," Wade asked her. "You seem sad."

She snatched her hand away. "Don't touch me," she whispered roughly. "If you ever put your mothafuckin hands on me again, I will kill you."

He chuckled. "You got it, gangsta, don't hurt me," he said throwing his hands up in the air. "You just look like you have a lot on your mind, and I was just checking on you."

"I do have a lot on my mind, but it doesn't have shit to do with you, Wade." She frowned. "Like I said, don't touch me."

"Did I do something to you?" he placed his hand over his heart. "If I did I apologize, all I want to do is get to know you. Make sure I put a smile on that face."

Damn he saying the right shit. Why is this happening to me? I'm trying to be faithful, I swear I am. "You didn't do nothing to me," she said rolling her eyes. "Just stay away." She focused back on the fight, which she wasn't interested in at all.

After Mike Tyson got knocked out in the eighth round, Marcel jumped up in defeat. "You fucking weak ass bastard," he yelled at the ring. "You owe me fifty G's mothafucka!"

Marcel was so angry he was cursing at the ring as if Mike could hear him, and more importantly, as if he gave a fuck. He was doing it to show off and get attention more than anything else, but he also hated being out of that amount of money.

Once they were out of the arena, and before they got into their rented limos, Jewels pulled her husband to the side. "Marcel, can we spend some quiet time in the hotel?" she looked into his eyes. "Maybe fool around a little bit?"

"Jewels, we going to a strip club tonight," he kissed her softly on the lips. "How about you come out with me," he wrapped his arms around her waist, "and get something to drink. I'm out of some cash so I need some fun."

"Marcel, all I want to do is chill with you, please baby," she said running her finger across the bottom of his chin.

As she was talking to him, he was looking over her head at the fine Tennessee females who were gawking at him. They'd never seen a black man with brown skin and gold curly hair before and he had them stuck.

"Jewels, look, you already got me." He separated from her so that she wouldn't block his flow with the ladies. "That should be good enough."

"What do you mean I got you?"

"You're my wife, Jewels, I mean, damn. What else you want?" He grabbed her finger hard again. "You got the ring already, relax." He let her finger go.

"Wade, I love you," she said softly.

The moment she realized that she called her husband another man's name, her heart stopped. But luckily for her this time, he was such a dog, that he didn't hear her.

Instead he continued to look at the females who were geeking over him. "How 'bout this, we'll hang out tomorrow for breakfast," he kissed her on the cheek. "I promise." He kissed her on the other.

After he was done with his wife, he walked around her and toward the women who thought he was either a model or a superstar. Instead of getting in the limousine and going to the strip club, she caught a cab to a little diner around the corner.

When she paid the cab, she was shocked to see Wade getting out of one of the rental cars. "What are you doing here?" she asked him. She walked toward the entrance.

"Marcel saw you leaving and told me to come watch you."

"Well I don't need nobody watching me, Wade. So go kill yourself." she walked inside of the restaurant and was seated immediately. He joined her without an invitation. "Please leave me alone, Wade."

"Unfortunately I can't do that."

The hostess sat two menus on the table and said, "Your waitress will be right with you."

When she walked away he said, "Why are you fighting it?"

"What do you mean fighting it?" she scanned the menu.

"I mean, it's obvious that you like me, and I like you. Instead of fighting it, we should just embrace what we have and start having fun together. Judging by the look on your face I can tell you need a good time. Let me do that for you."

She frowned. "I know you're not coming onto me." She slammed the menu down. "Do you know who I am?" she pointed to herself. "I am Mrs. Marcel Madison! My nigga is made, and you'll end up as fish food in one of his aquariums in our basement."

"I know who you are, Juliette, but do *you* know who you are?"

"What the fuck does that mean?"

"You are a woman who has married a man who is too stupid to know what he has. You are a woman who belongs to a little boy, when you deserve a real nigga like me. That's the only thing I know."

"What you mean you deserve a nigga like me? Don't you realize that if I called Marcel up right now and told him you coming onto me, that he would murder you? I'm somebody's wife!"

Wade took a cell phone out of his pocket, and slid it over to her on the table. "Call him, and tell him I want his wife. See if I give a fuck."

"And if I do, what do you think he'll do?"

"I don't care," Wade said softly. "Do you know that before I came over your house, on the first day I saw your face, that the plan was to tell him that although Gia was my peoples, that I didn't want to work with him?"

"Then why did you come over?"

"Because Gia begged me to at least talk to dude first. I know in the back of her mind she figured that Marcel could talk me into anything, like he talked her into anything, but my mind was made up that I wasn't interested in business dealings with him. That is until I saw your face."

Jewels' body was physically altered by his words and she hated herself for it. What a whore she was being! She was not only a married woman, but she also loved Marcel. Despite what her body was doing she knew that whatever was brewing between them could not go down.

"Wade—"

"You look so beautiful," he said interrupting her statement. "The color orange looks great on you by the way. I couldn't keep my eyes off of you all night. I'm trying to figure out what the fuck is wrong with your husband."

Damn, at least somebody noticed me. "You know what, I'm not hungry anymore," she said standing up.

"Well I'm going to take you to the hotel." He stood up too, and both of them moved toward the door.

"If you ever tell me how beautiful I am again, I'm going to tell Marcel," she said pointing in his face. "Do you understand?"

"And do you understand that there will come a time when I have to choose between Marcel and you. My question is, what do you think my decision will be?"

CHAPTER II

In The Courtroom:

"So we are to believe that you have never been unfaithful, despite the way you say he treated you at the Mike Tyson and Lennox Lewis fight?"

Jewels recalled the entire story about what happened at the fight, and left out Wade all together. She knew the moment she told him that another man was trying to court her, that they would try and find him, and deem her guilty.

"I said I love my husband and would never do anything so ridiculous," she responded.

"Are you sure, because if my wife was unfaithful, I would have to leave her and or find someone else who makes me happy."

"Well that's you but it ain't me," she said with a complete attitude. "Like I said I'm not that kind of woman! I would never be unfaithful. No matter how many times he did me wrong! At least I tried, before I realized he was never going to change. Even then I couldn't even look at another man."

The Truth:

Wade was in Jewels' house, in the library, going over plans for the next heist. Bet was over the house earlier, but had to leave to go to work. Although Jewels didn't want to admit it at first, she was happy Bet left. For some reason she found herself trying to spend some alone time with Wade, even though she knew it was wrong.

To make matters worse, Marcel was in Vegas and couldn't attend the meeting, which left the two of them alone. Marcel asked Wade to go over the plans with Jewels, and since she was great with explaining the details to Marcel, he would go over everything with her and the crew when he returned.

"You have to be sure to tell him that when he hits this location, that there are two cameras that point out to the street," he pointed on the map as he sat at the desk, and she sat next to him. Her knee brushed against his thigh, and he tried to remain calm. "So he needs to put something over his license plate, or they'll be a able to identify the van way before it even pulls up in front of the dealership."

Jewels took notes and said, "What about cameras in the back?" she pointed at a position in the rear. "At the door?"

"There are certainly cameras there, and a safe, but Gia knows how to break the code, because I've taught her everything." He sighs. "I really don't want you to go on this job since I'm not there, Juliette. Maybe you should sit this one out."

"What about your precious friend Gia? You care if she goes?"

He put the pen down and turned his chair so that he could look into her eyes. "You want to ask me something? If you do go ahead."

"Why would I ask you anything? You aren't my man."

"It's not because I don't want to be," he said.

"I hear you talking that good shit, Wade."

"We'll why do I detect a little animosity in your voice?" He winked.

She got up to grab a bottle of red wine off of the mantle, and poured both of them glasses. "I'm going to be real with you, I don't like your girl. It's mainly because Gia doesn't respect the fact that Marcel is a married man."

"Why do you say that?" He questioned, already knowing the answer.

"Why do you say that?" She repeated sarcastically. "Because she's out of town with a married man right now! While I'm here going over robbery plans with you. It's ridiculous at best," she continued yelling. "I mean why she gotta keep disrespecting the union?"

"Because you let both of them do it to you."

She handed him his glass of wine. "Why do you think you know so much about me, when I've told you nothing?"

"Because I know Gia," he sipped his wine. "She doesn't make a move unless she feels like she can get away with it. And because she feels she can, she will continue to push the limit. So either you or Marcel are giving her the green light, so either way both of them are wrong."

"So you're saying that she's taking advantage of me on purpose?"

"What do you think, Jewels, I mean be honest. You have slept with her with your husband many times before. At this point there is nothing you can say to either of them, because you have allowed them to go to the limit."

"I never put my mouth on her."

"But your bodies touched right?" he put the glass down. When he saw she wasn't speaking he stepped up to her. "Juliette, I'm not putting you down, I just want you to see what part you had in all of this. You have allowed this man to do these things to you and now he feels entitled."

She lowered her head. "I'm so frustrated, Wade." She placed the wine glass down on the desk. "If I leave him, where will I end up? I've never been with anybody before him. Marcel isn't just my husband, he's my mother, father, and everything."

Wade frowned because he didn't want to hear that shit. "Where are your parents?"

Up to this point, Jewels had never told anybody, not even her husband about her life in Honduras. Partially because she had received a social security number, a name, and an identity, because the government didn't know where she came from. As far as Marcel knew she was adopted and abandoned by her adoptive family. She didn't want to be looked down on by her husband, or anybody else. But for some reason, maybe it was the wine, she wanted to talk.

"I was born in San Pedro Sula—"

"Honduras," he responded, finishing her sentence. He looked at her with wide eyes. "Juliette, are you saying that you are from Honduras?"

"Yes, uh, how did you know?"

"My grandmother is from Honduras. She brought my mother here to America, before I was born, and we made a life for ourselves here. Damn, Juliette, we have more in common than I realized."

Mesmerized, Jewels went on to give him her entire life story, at least what she could remember. She talked about how her uncle sold her to an American to be raped, and how her friend was molested. Jewels even told him about how her mother gave her life for her, so that she could stay in this country without the burden of her. When she was done she was mentally exhausted, but grateful to him because she thought she'd never get it off of her chest.

Wade was everything Marcel wasn't, and Jewels was in awe. He was compassionate, a good listener, and even asked if he could do anything for her. She never met anybody who was from her country before that moment, and she felt a stronger connection to Wade than she ever had with Marcel. It was as if she were seeing him for the first time. She took in his long hair that was now tamed in long braids down his back; and the coffee cream color of his skin, along with his bad boy steez. How could she have not known? He screamed Honduran!

"But, Juliette, why are you putting yourself through this?" Wade said out of the blue. "Why are you living here, and allowing yourself to be emotionally abused? Now that I know you're from my country, I feel the need to be real with you even more. This nigga don't love you. I mean look at what he's doing! He in Vegas with another woman, a woman you hate at that! Why stay in his home?"

"Because I'm not strong enough yet," she sobbed. "I'm not strong enough to leave him, Wade and don't think I haven't tried."

Wade pulled her into his arms and allowed her to cry into his chest. He never took his hands off of her, as she broke down, and revealed her heart. Jewels spent thirty minutes crying over another man, and when she was done, it was his lips that caught her tears.

"I knew it was a reason I came here, Juliette," he said kissing her softly again. "Let me save you."

When their lips pressed tighter together, Jewels felt like he'd sucked the hurt and pain away from her body. "But this is wrong, Wade."

"Why it's gotta be wrong? You need me and I need you. It's destiny. And I'm going to stay with you, baby, until you are strong enough to walk away from this nigga and come with me. Because I don't need anybody to tell me what I already know, and that is that you belong to me."

After they embraced into a wide mouth kiss, and his tongue eased into her mouth, her clit tingled. He pulled her toward him, picked her up and gently placed her on the floor. Although Wade was kissing her passionately, out of respect, he hadn't advanced to the next level. It was Juliette who broke down the wall.

Jewels looked into his eyes and said, "Wade, I want this badly. Don't hold back on me when I need you the most. Please, make love to me."

"Are you sure, baby? Because I'll be sick if I find out you feeling guilty, when this nigga come home tomorrow."

"I know what I want, Wade, and what I want is you."

To prove her point, Jewels released the pearl buttons on her cream silk blouse. When her shirt opened, her cream bra was exposed, and her breasts peeked over the top.

Hungry for her, Wade removed one of her nipples and suckled on it softly, causing electricity to shoot down to Jewels' wet pussy. When he moved to the other nipple, and sucked on it a little harder, cream oozed into the seat of her panties, causing her pussy to slip and slide.

Ready to bask into the warmth of her flesh, he removed her bra before rubbing his hand slowly over her body. When he felt the time was right, he pushed her legs open and eased his manhood into her warm pussy.

Jewels hadn't expected Wade's dick to be so big, and he filled her up in ways that Marcel could never. Wade was a patient and considerate lover, unlike Marcel who needed an audience to last long in the bedroom. Wade was slow and methodical with his strokes, and she wanted it to last forever.

He was just about to cum, when Jewels looked into his eyes and boldly said, "I want to taste you, Wade. Will you let me?"

"What, baby? Are you serious?" he frowned. "I'm not going to treat you like some slut, Juliette. I care about you too much for that shit."

"Wade, please, for me. I'm a big girl. I can't get enough of you and I want to taste you. Let me, this is me talking not you."

To prevent him from denying her, she eased down, released his penis and he exploded into her mouth. Jewels flipped her clit ferociously while his dick, rested in her throat.

In The Foyer

"Baby, I'm home early," Marcel yelled in the foyer. He threw his keys down and they jingled as they fell onto the table. "I see Wade's car out front. He still here right? Because I wanna talk to him about the plans. We cut the trip early."

When she didn't answer, Marcel walked toward the library and opened the closed double doors. Wade was sitting on a chair in front of the computer, and Jewels was standing over top of him holding a clipboard.

"Hey, wifey," he said pulling her toward him roughly by the waist. The clipboard dropped to the floor. "I missed the fuck out of you! You ain't hear me calling?"

Without waiting on an answer, he pushed his tongue inside of her mouth, unknowingly tasting Wade's nut on her tongue. He was so self-centered and clueless, that he did not smell the sweet odor of their fuck session lingering in the air.

"I'm sorry, baby. I didn't hear the door."

"What's up, slim," Marcel said, giving Wade some dap. He swallowed his man's nut. "Thanks for coming over here at the last minute. So put me onto what ya'll been doing so far?"

"Uh...what you mean...uh?" he said.

"The robbery plans man," Marcel laughed. "What have ya'll gone through so far? I want all of the details, and don't leave nothing out. This is bound to be our biggest heist yet!"

CHAPTER 12

In The Courtroom:

"I'm having a hard time believing anything you say," the prosecutor said to Jewels. "Everything continues to sound like a complete fabrication."

He said that because Jewels told him how all of Marcel's friends came on to her, and how she never welcomed their advances. Nowhere in the story was there anything about Wade, and the first time they made love.

"I object," Adele said. "Prosecution is badgering the witness. It is not his job to make a decision if the witness is telling the truth or not. That responsibility belongs to the jury."

"Sustained," the judge said. "Please get to your question," he continued, giving him evil eyes.

"I'll repeat the question," he said, "Jewels, if your husband was as unfaithful as you claimed, why didn't you leave the marriage?"

"Like I told you before, my husband was and still is *everything* to me." She placed her hand over her heart for effect. "I was not about to leave the marriage when I dedicated my life to him. It's for better or worse, for richer or poorer, in sickness and in health. I stood by that."

"So you decided to kill him in cold blood like a dog in the park instead?"

"Objection, your honor," Adele yelled again.

"Howard, this is my final warning," the judge said frustrated with his unprofessional performance. "Now get to the point of your line of questioning."

"My apologies your honor." The prosecutor said. "Mrs. Madison, why didn't you leave or seek out another relationship, since it was so obvious that you were unhappy?"

"Because I still held onto hope that one day, things would get better."

The Truth:

Although Jewels was sleeping with Wade on the side, she was consumed with guilt. Her feelings were so strong for Wade that she was starting to question her love for Marcel all together. But when it became obvious that Marcel was going to do him regardless, she decided to finally give Wade her undivided attention, and that's exactly what she did.

Jewels had a tough week in her journalism class earlier in the day, and was looking forward to hanging out with Wade later on that night, at a hole in the wall lounge that Marcel would never be caught dead in. They had to be careful when they hooked up with one another.

She was talking to her best friend on the phone, trying to get ready. "Girl, why you sound so happy," Bet asked. "I mean it's one thing to be feeling a little better, but it's like you're floating on cloud nine over there."

"What you talking about?" she said looking at her body in the mirror. "I just made a decision to smile more, even when I don't feel like it. That's it."

"Bitch, don't play with me. I can already tell you're smiling from over here on the phone. What I want to know is why?"

She exhaled. "Let's just say that finally, I'm doing me in this marriage. Let's also say that I could give a fuck less what Marcel does any more. And lets just say that I have met somebody, who has helped me figure a few things out. With that said, I'll holla at you later, because I have to go and meet Mr. Destiny."

"You make sure you call me back too, because I want all of the details about this little date you're having! I hate when you cut me off without giving me everything when you know I live for it. I hate you!"

She giggled. "I love you too, bye, girl." She placed her phone down on her vanity.

Bet had proven to be true blue when it came to Jewels, and she felt grateful. Finally she had a friend who she could confide in about her life, and she didn't meet her through Marcel or his flunkies. But, Jewels wasn't sure how she felt about giving the specifics about her rendezvous with Wade. Her mother always told her that silence was best and she decided to remain mute, and not speak on her affair. At least not yet anyway.

After she hung up with Bet, and finished brushing her hair, she smoothed warm olive oil all over her skin. Marcel exited the bathroom with a towel wrapped around his waist. He walked up to her, and kissed her on the neck, as she looked at her reflection in the mirror. Lately when he touched her it felt as if a roach was crawling on her clitoris. His forehead banged against one of the extra large blue rollers, as he licked her neck.

"Have I told you that I love you today?" Marcel said, staring at her reflection. "Because sometimes I don't think I tell you enough."

It took everything in her power not to grab the gun under the bed, and shoot him in the face. "Yes," she said, hoping he didn't want to fuck. "You told me."

"Good, because you looking kind of sexy right now with your hair like this."

His stiff dick brushed against the crack of her ass and she wanted him to eat a bag of rocks, and leave her alone. Besides, she had plans to fulfill one of Wade's fantasies, and she didn't want to dirty her pussy up fucking with her husband.

"Thanks, baby," she smiled. "So what you doing tonight?" She was trying to get his eyes, and dick off of her and onto another subject.

"I'm trying to fuck you," he joked rubbing his hands over her breasts, like they were lumps of dough and he was about to make a pizza.

"Stop, Marcel," she said softly. "I'm going out, and I can't do that right now." She wiggled away from him.

His hands dropped and he frowned at her. "Fuck you mean stop? I'm your husband, what you sound like?"

"I don't want you to touch me right now," she said strutting away from him. "I'm entitled you know."

He sighed. "I know what this is about." He shook his head. "You mad because I'm going to *Stadium* again tonight. I told you that you can go with me and Gia if you wanted, but you said no remember? As a matter of fact she said she misses kissing that pink pussy of yours." he walked up to her and ran his hand over her steamy mound. "Why you don't let her?"

She jumped right before he stuck his finger into her pussy. "Marcel, I'm not mad, honestly. Go on out to the strip club and do you."

"I know you got an attitude. I can always tell. Since when do you not want me to fuck you? You practically walk around here with your pussy in your hand hoping I would at least pat it." He walked over to her.

His arrogance was paramount and she tried not to allow him to get to her. Not trying to get into an argument, so that she could see Wade she calmed down. "Marcel, I'm not mad, baby, I'm really not." She smiled. "You're right about me and the fact that I should appreciate everything you've done for me. From here on out, I'm going to start respecting you more, baby. I really am. And you are going to start seeing a major change in me." She kissed him on the nose and stepped off.

Marcel observed her and smiled. Finally she was seeing things his way, or so he thought. He loved her new attitude. Although he did what he wanted anyway, it was always best when he knew that she wouldn't be in his shit when he got home.

"You know what, with that attitude we gonna be together for a long time."

She slipped into her tiny black dress that exposed her cleavage. "Sure we are, honey." she grabbed her red Louis Vuitton clutch purse. "Sure we are." She slipped into her red pumps.

"I'm gonna be here waiting on you when you get home," he said looking at her release her rollers, causing her long flowing hair to wave down her body. *Damn my wife fine.* He thought.

She ran Ruby Woo lipstick by Mac over her full lips, puckered and said, "Have fun, baby." She walked out of the house, wearing no panties. *Because I know I will.*

123

An hour later Jewels was standing on the side of a city street, at night, holding her purse. She was walking up and down the small block, smoking a cigarette. She looked like a hooker, which was her aim. When Wade pulled up in his Maserati, and rolled his window down her heart fluttered. "You're very beautiful."

"Thank you," she said, trying to remain in character.

"So how much for your time?"

She seductively walked closer to the car, leaned on the window and said, "Fifty bucks for a blow job and seventy-five dollars for a fuck."

"For those prices I'll take both," he said. "Get in the car." She smashed the cigarette under her foot and got inside.

Wade pulled into a dark alley and parked. He wasn't sweet and compassionate like he usually was. "Get in the back, bitch."

Jewels quickly obliged. She crawled into the back seat, while on her knees, she raised the bottom of her dress so that it draped over the top of her ass. Then she placed both of her hands on the leather seat and lowered her waist, so that her pussy could open up like a flower.

Wade couldn't believe that her sexy ass was willing to do anything to get him off. He climbed into the back seat with her, and beat that pussy until it was juicy, wet, and dripping all over his seats. When he was finished, and he released all of his milk into her body, he kissed her on the back.

"You know I would kill somebody for you right?" he said kissing her on the nape.

She turned around, pulled her dress down and sat down. He pulled his pants up and sat next to her. She placed her hand softly on his face. "Wade, you have given me life again. I don't know what I would do if you weren't in my life. *Seriously.* You will never have to kill anybody for me, because as long as I'm alive I belong to you already. And like you said about choosing me when we were in Tennessee, I will choose you too."

He kissed her softly. "Why do I believe you?"

"Because you can see it in my eyes."

An hour later, they were in a hole in the wall lounge, dancing to the song *'Cry For You'* by Jodeci. As they danced on the floor, Jewels looked into his eyes and thanked God for bringing him into her world. Prior to Wade she didn't know what she was going to do with herself, and now all of her questions were answered. He was placed into her life to make her marriage work. Without Wade there would be no Marcel, and it was as simple as that.

When the song was over, they walked back over to their table to wait for their soul food. Wade had been holding something wrapped in gold and black wrapping paper, and finally he gave it to her.

"This is for you," he said grinning. "It's nothing big, but I wanted you to have it anyway."

She accepted the gift and smiled. "What's this for? You didn't have to get me anything, Wade."

"Just open it," he smiled sitting back into his seat. "Like I said, it's nothing huge, but it's from the heart all the same."

125

Jewels slowly tore off the beautiful paper, and looked at the gorgeous leather and gold journal in her hand. On the back of it her name was inscribed in gold lettering, and her jaw dropped. The words read, *'To my, Juliette. Use this to create your masterpiece."*

Jewels jumped up, flopped in his lap and kissed him sloppily on the lips. When she was finished she looked into his eyes again. "Wade, why do I deserve you? You listen to me, you inspire me, it seems like you do everything right. I don't understand."

"You deserve me because it's your time for happiness, Juliette. And I'm just ready to show you what your life can really be like."

"Marcel has bought me many gifts, but he has never, *ever*, done anything like this before. It's beyond thoughtful."

"Because you aren't supposed to be with him, Juliette. You never were. That's why he doesn't do things like this for you."

Her head dropped and she ran her fingers over the fibers of the leather journal. "I know, I know." She sighed. "You are telling me what I know already, but it's so hard taking a step forward and then out."

He moved her chin so that she was looking at him. "Juliette, when you gonna leave him to be with me? When you gonna be mine officially? Because I'm cool with this sneaking on the side for the time being, but I need more. I'm not a trick."

Jewels stood up, grabbed her book and walked to the other side. "Wade, please don't do this." She sat down.

"Please don't do what?" he leaned into the table. "Demand that you not sleep in this nigga's bed anymore?" he jabbed a finger into the table. "Is that what you asking me? I mean come on, Jewels." He sat back in his seat. "It's not like you even fucking the dude any-more. I can tell, because your body smells differently ever since you stopped dealing with him."

She was embarrassed. Marcel gave her a fresh case of gonorrhea before, and although she didn't fuck Wade while she had it, when it was clearing up they did make love, and he mentioned her special scent then.

"I might not be fucking him but he's still my hus-band."

Out of anger Wade laughed. "Yeah okay, Juliette. You can sit over there and play the good wife if you want too. But, I ain't buying the shit."

She frowned. "What the fuck is that supposed to mean?"

"You throwing up in my face that he's your husband, yet you're a fucking adulterer." Rage coursed through his veins and he let her have it. "You outside at night, acting like a whore, getting fucked in the back seat of my car! Don't tell me about your husband because I ain't trying to hear that shit."

Jewels' entire body trembled and tears exploded from the wells of her eyes.

Seeing how much he hurt her, Wade, immediately felt guilty and rushed to the other side of the table to con-sole her. He laid his hand on her arm. "I'm sorry, baby. I didn't mean that shit."

"Don't touch me," she said softly. When he didn't stop she yelled, "DON'T TOUCH ME!" People who were standing around looked at them, and he sat back in his seat.

"I know I was wrong for that shit, Juliette, and I'm so sorry, baby. I didn't mean what I said, but I'm just heated right now. It feels like I softened your heart, and made you realize that you deserve love, only for him to reap the benefits. I need you with me."

"That's not why I'm crying, Wade. It's not about what you said."

"Then what is it?"

"It's because before this day, I never thought you were capable of hurting my feelings." She stood up, grabbed her purse and book. "But I guess I was wrong."

She ran out of the lounge, leaving him alone.

He didn't follow.

When she finally made it home she was irritated when she saw Gia in her bed with Marcel. She was riding his dick, and their strokes were slow and passionate. They looked more like husband and wife, instead of she and Wade. As Juliette looked at them, carry on like they were a couple her heart broke. It wasn't even that she was jealous anymore. She was more embarrassed than anything else. She knew this was not the lifestyle she envisioned for herself, but she didn't know how to make things change.

Wanting to go to sleep, she walked up to the bed and said, "Marcel, I thought we were going to be alone tonight."

Gia turned around, flipped her long black hair over her shoulder and said, "Oh hey, Jewels, come to bed." She remained on top of her husband and reached for her.

She rolled her eyes. "I'm talking to my husband, bitch," she focused back on Marcel who was now looking at Jewels. "Marcel, please, can we be alone?"

"Jewels, get in bed. Gia not staying long anyway." He placed both of his hands on her waist and continued to pump into her body. "She has something to do in the morning."

"So you won't be alone with me, even though I'm begging you to?"

Marcel laughed her out. "You can either grab a titty or bounce. I don't know what else to tell you. But I do know this, I ain't cum yet."

CHAPTER 13

In The Courtroom:

Jewels told the prosecution exactly how Marcel continued to have other women in his bed, mainly Gia. Having sat on the stand and lied her ass off for awhile now, she was a master at avoiding questions on her own affairs, and exploiting the hell out of her deceased husband. Instead of telling the prosecution that she was with Wade that night, she said she went out with Bet, only to return home and see Gia and Marcel going at it again.

"You claim that Marcel was having an ongoing affair with Gia, if this is true, why would you allow it to go on for so long?" the prosecutor asked. "After all, that was your home not hers."

"Because I wanted to keep my marriage together, and I held onto the hope that at some point he would leave her alone, and come love me instead."

"Did that ever happen?"

Jewels began to daydream.

"Mrs. Madison, did it ever happen?

The Truth:

Jewels was on her way home, after leaving school. By all accounts she was truly having the worst week of her life. She and Wade stopped talking weeks ago, and when he would come over the house to discuss business with Marcel, he acted as if she didn't exist. A few times she called him, only for him to refuse to talk to her.

The only thing on Jewels' mind at the moment was going into her bathroom, locking the door, and soaking into her huge Jacuzzi bathtub, with a tall glass of wine in her hand.

When she turned onto the road leading to her house, she was irritated when she saw her driveway filled with cars. There were so many vehicles on the street, that some people resorted to parking in front of her neighbors home, and on her grass.

She parked her car, and angrily stomped toward the front door. This was it! She had it with Marcel! She had it with the infidelities! She had it with the wild parties, and she had it with her husband treating her worst than the whores who shared their bed. Today she was done, and something had to change.

She pulled her front door open, and stomped toward Marcel who was sitting on the recliner in the living room. The music was blasting, and it caused her an immediate migraine. On the left of Marcel was Gia, as usual, and to his right was another female she hadn't met before. Both of the bitches were sitting on the arm of the chair

"Marcel, I want these people out of my house," she screamed, to be heard over the music, placing her hand on her hips. "I'm sick of this shit!"

Feeling like she was stunting on him in front of his best friend and side candy he said, "Jewels, fall back before I hurt you." He rubbed Gia's thigh like it was Aladdin's lamp, and could grant him three wishes. "You know damn well who running things around here, and it damn sure ain't you. Don't get your feelings hurt up."

"Marcel, I want these people out of my house right now," she said huffing and puffing. "I'm not fucking around with you."

He looked up at her and saw something different, blinding rage. But he tried to pretend it didn't bother him. "Jewels, you heard what the fuck I said. Either grab a drink and dance or bounce!"

Irritated, she slapped the bitch to his right causing her to fall to her knees. With her out of the way she moved closer to Marcel, and hung over his head like a light bulb.

"I'm tired of being treated like this, Marcel," she screamed. "You are my fucking husband, and I deserve respect. So either you gonna start acting right, or you're about to lose me. I swear to God!"

Marcel balled his fists up and looked at them. Breathing heavily while looking on the floor he said, "Why the fuck would you just hit her? Huh?" Before she could answer he jumped up and towered above her, like the Statue of Liberty over New York. "Lately you been really feeling yourself and I'm tired of it."

"Do you really think I have to put up with this kind of shit? I don't have to deal with this anymore, Marcel."

"If you think you can find a nigga on earth who will do you better than me, prove it. Because you and me know that another nigga of my caliber don't exist. Now I don't know what's on your mind, but you better get yourself together before you find yourself out in the street, Jewels."

Jewels looked up at him and tears rolled down her face. The only thing she could say was, "Marcel, I'm done with you! It's over!"

"Yeah right, bitch. Talk that sweet shit tomorrow."

Jewels drove twenty miles on the other side of town to Wade's home. When she pulled into his driveway, she noticed two cars out front. Wade's Maserati and a red drop top Benz. She parked her car behind his, grabbed her purse and walked toward the front door. She was surprised when she saw it open, so she allowed herself inside without an invitation.

When she walked past the kitchen, she saw grocery bags sitting on the counter and slow music played softly from the speaker in the ceiling. When she bent the corner and saw a beautiful black woman with long hair kissing Wade, her heart rocked.

"Wade," she said softly walking into the living room.

At first he didn't see her, until his date stopped kissing him and focused on Jewels instead. Wade grabbed the remote and pointed it to the wall, causing the music to stop abruptly.

"What are you doing here, Juliette?" He threw the remote on the armchair. "Why are you in my house?"

"Get out," she told the girl, before answering Wade. "I need to talk to him alone, and I don't want you watching."

She smirked and looked at Wade. "Who is this chick, Wade?" she pointed at her. "Because I thought you said you were single."

He looked at Juliette.

"It's the love of his life," Juliette said, speaking up for him, "and I'm not about to allow you or anybody else to take him away from me. So get the fuck out."

The woman looked at Wade and waited for his reply. Instead of putting Jewels in her place he said, "You heard her, Marilyn. Get your things and bounce. I'll get up with you later."

The gorgeous woman angrily snatched her red Gucci purse off of the counter and bumped Juliette's shoulder on her way out of the door. Jewels didn't flinch an inch, and her gaze remained on him.

Slowly she walked up to him, wondering if she still had the right to hold him. *To touch him.* After all, the last time she saw Wade, she walked out on him at a lounge. Had he forgiven her yet? "I'm sorry, Wade."

He walked past her, and moved toward the groceries on the counter. He unloaded the bags starting with the vegetables. "What you want, Juliette? You married remember? And I'm not your husband, like you threw up in my face the last time I saw you."

"I want you back, Wade. Can I have you?" She asked, sounding so elementary like, even though it rocked his heart.

"No," he said placing the broccoli in the vegetable drawer in his refrigerator. "You want to be with a nigga who doesn't do you right, then go back over to your house and join the party. We through."

Her eyebrows rose. "You knew about the party?"

"Yes," he said placing milk into the fridge door. "He invited me."

"Then why didn't you tell me, Wade? I came home thinking I was going to get some rest, and saw that shit going down at my crib."

"I don't talk to you no more remember? I'm tired of this shit anyway, Juliette. I'm tired of the games you playing with me. You fucking my head up right now, and I don't need this shit anymore."

Juliette walked up to him. "Wade, please don't leave me now." She rubbed her hand over his chest. "I acted weakly, scared and dumb. And I let you get away from me, for a nigga who could care less."

"Don't call yourself dumb, Juliette." He walked away from her again. She was driving him crazy, and her sex appeal was turned up.

"Then what else would you call it? I'm a woman who allowed the best thing to ever happen to her get away." She walked up behind him and rubbed his back. He turned around and faced her again. "If I'm not dumb then what am I?"

"You confused, and I get that, Juliette, I really do, but I will never, *ever*, allow myself to be placed in a situation like that again. I'm over you now."

Her heart dropped into the pit of her stomach. She was about to believe him until she remembered how he told the girl to kick rocks. "You not over me, nigga. You hear me?" she grabbed his shirt collar, and stared into his eyes. "You not over me! I have never wanted to kill a man in all of my life, but I will kill you dead, Wade, if you ever try to leave me. Deep in my heart I have the capacity for murder, I know it."

Although he knew he should've been frightened, he couldn't understand why his dick was rock hard. "You don't know what you saying, Juliette."

He walked over to the refrigerator to grab a beer.

"I do know what I'm saying," she said following him. "I'm saying that you are the one that I want to be with for the rest of my life, and I finally get that now. You know what, when I went home and saw Marcel with Gia and some other bitch, I—"

"So that's the reason you came over here?" He asked cutting her off. "Because that nigga hurt you again?"

"No, that's not it. Let me finish, baby," she said softly. "When I went home and saw him with all of them

135

bitches, the only thing on my mind was you, and how I let you go for him. I'm not doing that again, Wade."

"You saying everything I wanna hear, but if I take you back where does that leave us?"

"It's up to you, Wade." She walked up to him again, removed the beer from his hands and sat it on the counter behind him. She pressed her body against his. "It's all up to you."

"Don't say it's up to me, because you know what I want from you."

"Like I said, it's up to you, I mean, do you still want me? After all, you did just have another girl in here."

"She was somebody who I passed time with. I'm not gonna lie, she didn't deserve that shit we just did to her, but you got my mind wrapped up, and forced me to make a decision, so for the moment I chose you."

"I don't mean to have your mind wrapped up," she said placing her head over his heart. His beat was calm and steady. "I'm ready to be yours, Wade. If you'll still have me." His heartbeat sped up.

"Are you really ready, Juliette?"

"I am, all I need you to do is give me three months to ease out of his house."

"Why not now?"

"Because my entire life is over there. And I want to start putting some things up that I don't want to leave behind. When I finally bounce, I don't want him to know that I'm gone."

He looked down at her. "You got one month, Juliette. If you take a day more I won't be here for you anymore. Do you understand?"

"I do."

CHAPTER 14

In The Courtroom:

While the prosecutor, and the courtroom looked at her with disapproving eyes, she thought about Wade a little more. She didn't care that they didn't believe she wasn't unfaithful. She knew she didn't have to convince them of her lies. It was the jury who had to see her as pure and innocent. And although she knew it was wrong to be with another man, when Wade came into her marriage, she'd never been happier.

The Truth:

Marcel, Jewels, Wade and the gang were all at the Stadium Strip club in DC. Marcel had five thousand dollars worth of ones on the table with him in the VIP room, and a bunch of beautiful women surrounded him. He was on top of the world, until he realized unlike the many times in the past when Jewels bugged him about spending time with her, now she was giving him his space. Where was she?

After the fight they had at the party, Jewels came home and begged him to take her back. He did with no problem, after laying down the groundwork. Number one; he could stay out for as long as he wanted. Number two; he could do whatever he wanted. Number three; she couldn't question him about shit. She agreed with his rules and didn't so much as look his way when Gia shared his bed, or he didn't come home until the next day. In fact the last time Gia was in the bed with them, Jewels who just fucked Wade, took to reading a book. She could care less what they were doing or how they did it, and they were right next to her.

When Marcel scanned the strip club for his wife, he glanced down the VIP room and saw her laughing it up with Wade in a corner. Jewels' back was against the wall, while she held onto her drink, and he was in front of her like they were standing at a locker in high school.

"What you thinking about," Gia asked whispering in Marcel's ear. "I've never seen you turn your head before when *Wet Ice* stepped on the stage."

"I ain't thinking about nothing," he lied, still staring at Jewels and Wade.

"Then why you looking all funny?"

"Do me a favor, go get my wife," he directed sipping a bottle of *Ace of Spade* champagne from the spout.

"Your wife," she giggled. "Who you talking about? Miranda? Nessie? Or Wet Ice?"

Irritated he said, "Who the fuck did I say I do too?"

Gia frowned. She knew as well as he did that Marcel didn't respect the marriage, or titles. "You talking about Jewels?"

"Go get her, Gia, before I fuck you up in here," he said with an attitude.

Gia reluctantly walked over to Jewels who was irritated the moment she saw Gia's face. "Your husband want you," she said dryly.

"For what?" She giggled, with the residuals of a smile left on her face, due to something Wade just said.

"Because he asked for you. How 'bout you ask him about all the details, instead of bothering me with them." She walked off mad she had to step to her in the first place.

When Jewels and Wade walked over in Marcel's direction, Marcel was immediately irritated. He sent for her, not him.

"What's up, baby," Jewels said softly, sipping her drink.

"I was wondering why ya'll not over here looking at strippers with me."

"You know that's your thing not mine," Wade said, eyes still on Jewels and the cleavage spilling out of her blouse. *Damn she fine*. He thought.

Wade wasn't trying to play Marcel, because he did this type of thing all the time and Marcel never cared or noticed, until now.

"So what, you don't like beautiful women no more?" Marcel questioned, taking another sip of Ace.

Wade unconsciously looked at Jewels again and smiled. Marcel caught this glimpse and it took everything in his power not to fracture his jaw.

A little buzzed, and not in control of his words Wade said, "I love beautiful women, but can't nothing in this club fuck with your wife."

"Wade," Jewels blushed, pushing his chest, running her hand softly downward.

Again, she did this type of thing all the time too, but Marcel never cared. His mind was always on himself, and his bevvy of bitches. No wonder she wasn't tripping no more, this nigga had come out of nowhere, and swooped her off of her feet.

"Stop trying to get my head all puffed up," Jewels continued, blushing.

"I'm just being real," Wade looked at Marcel. "Your husband is one lucky man."

"You probably say that shit to a lot of people," she said taking Wade's hand, and walking back over to the corner. She did all of this without so much as even waving bye to Marcel, who stood in the middle of the floor looking stupid. They carried the dog shit out of him.

"Ain't nobody trying to fill your head up with a bunch of lies," Wade added, as they made it back to their corner.

Without even realizing it, due to being lost in each other's conversation and eyes, they just set off a ticking time bomb. Marcel was so enraged about what was obviously brewing between one of his gang members and his wife, that he couldn't enjoy the flesh show any more. His entire life he always wanted the thing that wasn't his, instead of the thing he had. He wasn't worried about Jewels when he had her heart. But now that it was gone, he had major problems with the scenario.

Two hours later they were in a late night diner. Although everyone else was drunk and enjoying themselves, Marcel couldn't help but focus on Wade and Jewels, who was so involved in each other that they were physically leaning on one another.

He didn't know how or when, but he had all intentions on shutting that situation down.

CHAPTER 15

In The Courtroom:

"Juliette, you mentioned in your previous testimony that you never got violent with Mr. Madison," the prosecutor stated.

"Yes," she said wondering where he was going with his line of questioning again. "I never...I mean...I didn't hurt him."

"Who is Alger Ness?" the prosecutor blurted out.

Juliette moved around in her seat, trying to get comfortable. She could still smell the odor from the urine on her clothes from when she pissed on the stand. "He was my next door neighbor." She clasped her hands together.

"Was he living in the neighborhood the entire time you were married to Mr. Madison? This neighborhood that you failed to tell the court about?"

"We were able to afford to live in the neighborhood, after Marcel saved his money, and started working in construction on the side. I forgot to mention that earlier, I'm sorry."

"Construction huh? In a million dollar home?"

"Yes," she nodded, before swallowing loudly.

"Well who burned down that million dollar home, on the day Marcel was murdered?"

Jewels was stuck because she didn't know he knew anything about their house, and she certainly didn't think he would suspect her of arson. After all, the day Marcel was murdered, and the house was burned, she was locked up.

"I don't know," she answered honestly. "Maybe it was someone who had something to hide, like one of his many lovers."

"It just seems so convenient that everything regarding Marcel's life is gone away too."

"And all I can say is that it wasn't me," Jewels said more firmly.

"To repeat my question, did Alger Ness live in the same neighborhood?"

"Yes he did," she said wiping sweat off of her forehead.

"If you were never violent with Mr. Madison, how do you explain the sworn statement that we received from him?" he looked at the paperwork in his hand, and flipped the page. "In it he stated that you tried to kill your husband just before he was actually murdered."

The Truth:

Juliette came home from just meeting with Wade. She was about to grab some clothes, and meet him back at his house. But when she opened the front door, and walked into her room, Wade was the last thing on her mind. The pain she felt at the moment was blinding. Because there in the bed, with her husband, was her only friend Bet. Along with Gia and another woman she didn't know.

"Oh my, God," Jewels said covering her mouth. She dropped her purse on the floor. "I can't believe, please don't tell me...why is this happening?"

"Juliette, I am so sorry," Bet said jumping up off of the bed, revealing her naked body underneath. "I didn't know you were coming home. Marcel, why didn't you tell me," she yelled at him. "You did this shit on purpose didn't you?"

Jewels was seeing black. This was the final straw. If Marcel wanted war, then that's exactly what he was going to get. After all, this was beyond foul. He knew that she was the only person that was in her corner, and he slept with her anyway. Juliette had no idea that Marcel peeped the interaction between her and Wade brewing, and decided to hit her in the jugular.

"Bet, you were my best friend, my only friend," she placed her hand over her thumping heart. "Why would you want to hurt me like this? I don't understand."

"I'm sorry, Jewels," she jumped into her jeans. "I didn't want to tell you, because I knew you wouldn't understand, but me and Marcel go way back." She put on her shirt. "He dumped me, and I hadn't seen him again until he was marrying you. I'm so sorry."

Jewels heard something snap in her brain, and suddenly she walked purposefully toward the kitchen. She was gone for a second before she returned to the room with the largest butcher knife known to man.

The first person she went at was the bum bitch Bet. Jewels caught her with a slash to the arm, opening up her flesh like ground beef in a plastic pack. Blood spewed everywhere but Jewels could not be stopped. While Bet was trying to run out of the bedroom, she caught her again by stabbing the middle of her back.

"LEAVE ME ALONE," she screamed, running out of the house.

When Bet was gone, she went swinging after Gia with the knife. She wasn't going for the arm on her. She wanted to rearrange that little Italian face. But Marcel jumped in front of her, protecting her with his body.

"You better not cut her face," Marcel warned. "If you fuck her face up I'll kill you."

Jewels finally saw the kind of man he really was. There she was broken hearted by his betrayal with her best friend, and the only thing he could say was to not destroy his precious friend's face. She hated him even more in that moment, and she knew she was done with him forever.

Suddenly she started chasing him with the knife. At first Marcel didn't budge, until he looked into her eyes and saw murder. He ran toward the foyer, and then out the front door with nothing on his body but the hair on his dick. When they finally made it by the water fountain, Jewels kept yelling and swinging the knife, while trying to stab him. This is when her neighbor Alger Ness witnessed the event from his home.

"Bitch, if you cut me I will kill you," Marcel yelled pointing at her with his right index finger, while trying to cover his dick with his left hand. "I'm not fucking around with you, Jewels."

"You have hurt me for the last time, Marcel," she yelled pointing the blade at his face. "The last fucking time, and I'm finally done with you forever."

"Yeah, right, bitch, what you gonna do without me?"

"Everything! Starting with living my life how I want to. You never loved me, and the only reason you kept me around was so that you can say you did this for me, and that for me. But you know what, I don't care about those things anymore, because I found something greater."

"Sure you did," he laughed. "But you forgot about one thing, Bet told me how accustomed you have become to the luxurious lifestyle that I provided for you. You can't leave me even if you wanted to, because nobody can afford you but me." He was referring to Wade. "And I do mean nobody."

"We'll see about that."

At Wade's House

"It's cool, baby, I got you now," Wade said as he rocked her in his arms. They were in the bed lying down. "You don't have to worry about anything anymore. And stop letting the dumb shit that, that nigga did to you tonight, fuck up your head."

"I know but you should've heard him, Wade. He slept with my best friend and he didn't give a fuck. And then he had the nerve to tell me that if I cut Gia's face, he would kill me. Fuck the fact that you cheated on me, you gotta fuck my best friend too?"

"I know this hurts, Juliette, but old girl was foul anyway, so he did you a favor. You gotta look at this as a blessing in disguise."

"I know I do, Wade," she looked up into his eyes. "I can't believe that I almost allowed him to take you away from me. What would I have done if you weren't in my life?"

"You came around just in time now didn't you?" he winked.

"You know I did," she laughed. "And listen at you sounding all cocky and shit. You probably willed this into our existence didn't you?"

"As much as I wanted to see you with me, I would've never willed you to go through anything like that, Jewels."

"I know, baby," she said.

"But we still have something else to discuss," he said seriously running his fingers through her long hair.

"Aw, shit, be easy on me, Wade, I had a rough day."

"I know, and you know I don't want to make it rougher. But, we still have to talk."

"What's the problem?"

"I need to know what you going to do tomorrow. Being here with you feels great, but what about tomorrow? Are you going to be with me or not? Or are you going to get on the phone with that nigga, and leave again?"

"Wade, I'm with you," she said looking up at him. "I don't want to go through that shit no more. I can't deal with the pain from a nigga I didn't even love."

"How do I know for sure?"

"You mean besides the fact that I'm never going back to his house again, because he slept with my best friend?"

"Yeah, besides that," he responded, although pleased that she was finally making master moves.

"You mean besides the fact that I love you so much, and I never want to lose you?"

"Yeah, more than that," he grinned.

"You mean besides the fact that I'm filing for divorce?" His heart rocked, and his eyes widened. She knew she had him. "Do you believe me now?"

He smiled and fucked her better than she ever had been in her entire life.

CHAPTER 16

In The Courtroom:

"If we are to believe you, you lost your temper because he slept with your best friend, and you didn't try to stab him?"

"You can believe me because that's what happened. I walked in from school, only to see him in the bed with my best friend. I got mad, and chased him out of the house with a knife." She didn't tell them that she stabbed Bet, or that she went to Wade's house afterwards. "But he wasn't injured, because I decided that it wasn't worth it."

"So where did you go that night?"

"I got a hotel room," she lied, as a tear fell from her eyes. "You have to understand, I didn't have any family or friends outside of Marcel. I had absolutely nobody to turn to. Nowhere to go."

"I bet," the prosecutor said under his breath. If anybody asked his opinion he would tell them that he hated Jewels with a passion, and didn't believe anything she said. In school beautiful women like her shitted on him all of the time, and he was taking the case personal. "So you said that you filed for divorce because you couldn't be with him anymore?"

"Yes."

"How did he react to the filing?"

"Not too good. Not too good at all."

The Truth:

"Baby, I don't know how you do it," Wade said to Jewels, as she sat across the table from him, smiling her face off. "Your cooking is the best I've ever had in my life."

"But your mother is from my country too. I'm sure she cooks way better than me."

"My mom got over here and all she wanted to do was make American meals. I love her dearly but it's not the same." He places some more of the dish into his mouth. "What is it?" It resembled a fajita.

"Well, since I haven't been back to Honduras, I decided to teach myself a few meals. So what you're eating is called Pupusa."

"What's in it?" he ate some more.

"Really just cheese, cilantro, cumin and masa harina," she placed another piece on her plate and sat down. "It didn't take me long to make, but I wanted you to have something from our country."

"Masa what?" he questioned, referring to one of the ingredients.

Although she was certain that Wade was sincerely interested in what she was cooking, it was his love and his attention that reminded her that she was wise for choosing him over Marcel.

"It's called Masa harina, it's like a dough," she sipped her red wine. "And it's the outer part of the meal, but I'm so glad you like it." She wiped the corners of her mouth with the white cloth napkin.

"I love it," he said winking at her, eating the rest. When he was done he sat his fork down and gave her a serious look. "I wanna talk to you about something serious, Juliette."

She swallowed and tried to rid herself of the lump forming in her throat. "Sure, what you wanna talk about?" *Please don't tell me you don't love me anymore already.*

"I think we should move to Atlanta."

She coughed and wine flew out of her mouth. "Atlanta," she wiped her mouth. "Why, Wade?"

"Because everything about this city and place reminds me of your past, and him. And, Juliette, I don't want to be a part of your past anymore. I want to remain a part of your future. And we do that by starting our own memories together."

"You are my future, haven't I shown you that I'm willing to give it all up for you?"

"It's not about that, Juliette. It's about the fact that you had a life here with Marcel. Your husband. And I don't want the possibility of him being so close, to interfere in what I'm trying to build with you. Now I got enough money saved up to buy us a beautiful home. Let's get out of here."

"I don't know, I think it seems premature. It's not like Marcel has even called me."

"First let me say that I know for a fact that you love me, and I'm not questioning that. So if I gave you the impression that I doubt your loyalty, I'm so sorry. But I know that nigga, and men like him don't like being beaten. Whether he contacted you or not is not the question. He will fight to get you back."

"You call me leaving him being beaten?"

"I call it a knockout. I want to marry you, Juliette, and he won't be able to see you with my last name. In his mind it's just a matter of time before you come back to him, once you realize what you lost."

Her heart beat rapidly in her chest and her forehead moistened. "Wade, I wanna marry you too, eventually, but first I have to get divorced."

"And I know that, but that's the plan I'm thinking of, to relocate. You divorce him and marry me. With you as my wife I won't lose. Don't you see what I'm saying?"

"How come I feel like you're trying to pressure me like he did?" Jewels got up from the table, and walked to the bar in his living room.

"If I'm giving you that impression I'm sorry." When he saw her preparing to make a stiff drink, with a trembling hand he said, "sit at the bar, Juliette, I got you." She took a seat and he prepared an extra strong martini for her. "Baby, these are just things we should consider, and are not meant to upset you." He handed her the drink, and made himself a glass of vodka straight up.

"I know we are going to have a life together, and a long one too," she said.

"See we already agree on some things." He downed his drink.

"I just don't wanna make a mistake again by moving so quickly, Wade."

"So you think you can make a mistake by moving with me?" he slammed the glass on the bar.

"Of course not, Wade," she sighed. "But what's wrong with taking things slow?"

"Nothing, baby, but I want to claim my prize. And I want to do it now. So if I'm pressuring you it's just because now is the time. Once you get divorced, and we move away into a nice beautiful home in Atlanta, then I won't worry about anything else. Because I'll know that you are all mine."

Jewels thought about what he was saying. Yes she wanted to allow the divorce to be settled first. And yes she wanted to take some time to make sure that Wade was actually the one she wanted to spend the rest of her life with. But she also realized something else. If Wade were to walk out on her again, simply because she wasn't ready to fully commit, she would be by herself forever. Ever since her mother died she experienced extreme bouts of loneliness, when it didn't have to be that way anymore. Wade was saying he was there for her.

"You're right baby, whatever you think is best I'm with." She slid off of the barstool and walked behind the bar to embrace him. "Besides, I know in my heart that you are the one for me. I felt it the very first moment you looked into my eyes."

When there was a loud disturbance outside, and they heard a male's voice, Wade rushed toward the living room window. He pushed the thick hunter green curtains back and peered outside. There in the front of his lawn was Marcel's Bentley.

Wade lost it. "I'm about to unleash on this nigga," he yelled grabbing his gun off of the table, and sticking it into the back of his jeans.

"Please don't go out there," Jewels said already knowing it was Marcel.

"I'm not gonna hide in my own house like some bitch, Juliette. And I know you don't want a man like that either, so don't fool yourself. Now if the nigga wanna see 'bout me, I'll call him on it." He kissed her on the lips. "Don't worry, I'm coming back."

Wade pulled the door open, and approached his car. Marcel was leaning against the car door drinking a bottle of vodka.

"You want a drink?" he raised the bottle in his hand.

"Fuck that shit, nigga," Wade said slapping the bottle. "What you doing here?"

"So that's how you do it?" he pointed the bottle toward Jewels who was looking out the window. "You come into my house, take my wife and put her up in your crib?" he downed some more liquor. "What part of the game is this, man? I put you on. Where's the fucking loyalty?"

"You didn't put me on. You couldn't even take care of your own crew, and keep things going. It was me who legitimized your business. *I* put *you* on, nigga!"

"I thought we was cool, man," he said swaying from left to right.

"I never fucked with you, Marcel. Just so you know. The only reason I helped you for as long as I did, was because you had *my* wife in your possession, and I needed to correct that. I've done that already, and now we have no more business to discuss."

Jewels was now standing in the doorway. Sweat poured down her face as she waited for the verdict. Would Wade live or not? She saw the murder in Marcel's eyes as he looked at Wade and her, and she didn't see the situation ending well.

"You the foulest of niggas."

"And why the fuck is that? Because I didn't let you abuse her anymore?"

"Because you knew she was my wife. I don't give a fuck if I had her sitting in the doghouse every night, what I did with her was none of your business."

"As far as I can recall, that's exactly how you treated her. You didn't care that all she wanted to do was love you. You didn't care that all she wanted you to do was spend some time with her. You not husband material, my man and that's cool. The thing is I am, and I'm going to raise a family with her, and make her happy."

"Jewels, come here so I can talk to you," he walked around Wade and toward Jewels. "Come out here and talk to me, baby."

With a firm hand to the chest Wade stopped him. He looked back at Jewels and said, "Juliette, go into the house, sweetheart. I'll be in, in a second." He looked back at Marcel. "You don't control that no more, my man. That thing belongs to me."

Marcel gritted on him when he saw how quickly Jewels obeyed. "I'm going to kill you for this shit." Marcel chest bumped him and pointed in his face. Although he was violating, Wade didn't flinch. "Do you hear me, nigga? I'm going to murder you for this shit."

"You do what you gotta do," he replied as he reached behind his back, and placed his hand over the handle of his gun. Before he could use it Marcel jumped into his car and sped away from the scene. Leaving a dirt cloud behind him.

When Wade went back into the house, Jewels was a nervous wreck. It broke his heart to see her so nervous. He closed and locked the doors, and approached her where she sat on the kitchen floor. He got on his knees and looked at her.

"Juliette, don't be afraid. I need you to know that I can always protect you."

"I'm trying not to be, Wade, but I feel so bad for him. He looked...he looked...miserable."

He frowned because he realized that she still had feelings for him, until he remembered that at some point she had to have cared for the man. No matter how trifling he was. "Are you trying to back out on me?"

"Fuck no," she replied, wiping her tears away. "What I look like backing out on you?" she placed both of her hands on his face. "You're my everything, Wade." She kissed his lips. "It's just that I saw the look in Marcel's eyes." Her hands dropped in her lap. "I saw it before after I watched him kill a man in front of me. I got a feeling that he's going to try his hand pretty soon, and we must prepare."

"If you really feel that way, then let's move to Atlanta in a couple of weeks."

She giggled a little and wiped the tears away from her eyes. "You are dead serious about making the move aren't you?"

"Dead serious."

"Do you know a good area for us to relocate? Because I don't know nothing about Atlanta, Wade. I'm going to be trusting you with everything."

"And that's all I want you to do, Juliette. And I know Marcel scared you when he came over here, but he ain't no gangster. He would never try me like that, because he know what kind of people I roll with. It would be a bad move for him, trust me."

"Are you sure?" she asked.

"I'm positive." He kissed the inside of her hand. "Trust me, baby, with me you're safe. Don't worry about a thing."

CHAPTER 17

A Week Later

The Truth:

Jewels was riding Wade's dick while looking down at him. Surprisingly he was right when it came to Marcel. Not only did Marcel back off, he didn't bother to come over and see about her anymore. Although he had yet to sign the divorce papers, she knew it was just a matter of time before the marriage would be dissolved, and she could move on as Mrs. Juliette Wallace.

"Why your pussy gotta be so tight," he said pushing into her slowly, so that he could prolong the orgasm. "It feels like you gripping my dick tightly with your hand."

She grinned, and bucked her waist again. She dropped her head backwards and allowed her long luscious hair to touch his thighs. It was feathery soft. After teasing him she looked at him again and winked. "Why your dick so stiff and warm?" she bit her bottom lip.

He chuckled. "You be talking that mob wife shit." He pumped a little harder into her body. "I still can't believe you all mine. You don't know how good it feels not to have to worry about another nigga in the picture."

"And you don't know how good it feels not to have to worry about another woman. I was so tired of that lifestyle, Wade. Real tired of it. And now knowing that every morning when I get up, that I don't have to compete for my man's love, makes me stronger, and want to be a better woman."

He fucked her until he reached his orgasm, and she reached hers. When they were done, she said, "I want to show you something." She hopped off of him and grabbed the journal he gave her. Then she placed the book on the bed, and stuck his dick back into her body where it belonged.

He shook his head, loving that move. "You the sexiest bitch I ever met in my life, on some serious shit. How you come back over here like nothing happened, and put my joint back inside of you?"

"Because it's never supposed to leave me." She handed him the book. "Now read what I got so far."

Wade took the book and flipped page after page. His eyes widened as he read Jewel's half written story. "Damn, Juliette, this is really good. I knew you had talent, but I didn't know it was like this."

"You just saying that."

"No I'm not, baby. You really got talent," he said honestly.

"You think it's good enough to be published?"

"Fuck yeah, now you got me wanting to read the rest. You gotta hurry up and finish it."

She was going in for another round with Wade, when suddenly she felt her stomach churn. Scared she would vomit all over him, she hopped up, and dashed to the bathroom. She closed the door, dropped to her knees and placed both hands on the cool toilet bowl. She was throwing up for a minute before Wade knocked on the door.

"Baby girl, what's going on in there?"

"Let me see," she said going under the sink to grab a box of pregnancy tests. "I'll be out in a second, don't worry."

Juliette kept a box of pregnancy tests with her, since her period was so irregular, she could never tell if she was pregnant or just skipping a cycle. After taking the test, fifteen minutes later, she came out of the bathroom carrying the test, and wearing a smile on her face.

"Aw shit, what you over there grinning about?" he asked. "And get your fine ass back in this bed. I'm not through with you yet."

Jewels sat on the edge of the bed and then looked over at him. "Wade, I don't know how you're going to take this, but here." She handed him the test and a drop of her piss hit his upper lip.

He laughed, and instead of getting mad licked it off.

"Ugghh," she laughed. "That was gross!"

"Nothing coming out of your body is gross," he winked. "But I already know what you gonna tell me."

"And what is that?" she said slyly.

"You pregnant," he smiled, waving the test.

"Yeah...but how you know...I didn't?"

"Your body has been filling out, and I notice everything about you." Suddenly he seemed sad and he looked away from her. "I just got one question for you, before I get too excited."

She crawled next to him. "What is it?"

"Am I the only man you slept with? I mean, I know you were living in that house, but are you sure you didn't fuck Marcel again?"

"Of course not," she said truthfully. "I hadn't slept with him in months. I decided at least three months ago that I wasn't fucking with him no more, and I stood my ground. So this baby growing inside of my body is yours...it's ours." She rubbed her stomach.

He embraced her, and kissed her passionately. He couldn't keep his hands off of her if he tried. "Damn, Juliette, shit with you just keeps getting better."

"You sure you want this with me? The baby that is?"

"Of course I want the baby," he yelled. "Man, there ain't nothing that we can do together that I won't love. Just as long as you don't leave me."

"Never," she said looking into his eyes. She sat up and looked down at him. "And now that you know I'm pregnant, let the cravings begin." She said rubbing her hands together. "I want you to go get me some beef tacos from Taco Bell, because I got the munchies."

He sat up straight in bed, shook his head and laughed. "You and them fucking tacos."

"What can I say," she shrugged, "I just love 'em."

Although he talked a lot of shit, he went to get the food. While he was gone Juliette ran a nice warm bath, and stayed inside of it for two hours. When she couldn't get any more hot water, she realized Wade hadn't come home yet. When she got out of the tub and called him five or six times, he still didn't answer the phone. Fear washed over her because she immediately felt that something was wrong.

She decided to leave him a message. "Wade, I'm really worried about you. Can you at least call me and tell me that you're okay? Please, baby."

Another hour passed and still she heard nothing from Wade. She became a nervous wreck and even resorted to calling the police. They said because he was a grown man, and she was not his wife, she had to wait for 48 hours to report him as missing.

● ● ●

A week passed and so much had changed, including the fact that due to worry, she lost the baby. Next to her mother being murdered before her eyes, it was the most devastating event she ever experienced. Barren and distraught, she was on the verge of a mental breakdown.

When the front door opened a few days later, she quickly jumped out of bed and ran to the living room.

"Wade, baby, is that you," she smiled.

The smile on her face was wiped off when she bent the corner. Instead of seeing Wade, she was looking into the face of her angry husband. Although he looked fly in his crisp blue jeans and his nice leather jacket, he was the ugliest thing she'd ever seen in that moment. She didn't look too good herself. Jewels' hair was all over her head, and she hadn't bathed in over seven days.

Instead of saying anything to her, he threw an odd necklace her way. She caught it, and when she looked down, she saw it was made with Wade's fingers. It dropped out of her hands. She would know his finger anywhere, because there wasn't a place on his body she didn't worship.

She looked up at him with hate. "No...no...no! Say you didn't, Marcel! Say you didn't do it!"

"I think you thought it was a game when I said you are my wife." He approached her slowly. "Once you made a decision to marry me, it was for better or worse." He chuckled to himself. "This is the bad part." He winked. "Jewels, don't you understand, I will never let you go, and I will never let another nigga come in and take you away from me. I thought you knew that already." He walked up to her and slapped her in the face, before punching her in the stomach, causing her to drop to her knees. He grabbed a fistful of her hair, pulled her head up and said, "That's for your pussy smelling again. I told you what I'd do if I ever smelled you again." He let her hair go, and wiped his hands together, as if he was trying to get rid of dirt. "Now do yourself a favor, and go throw some clothes on." he walked toward the door, and looked back. "And, Jewels, if you have me waiting more than five minutes, I'ma come back in here, and blow your fucking brains out all over this dead niggas crib."

CHAPTER 18

In The Courtroom:

Since Jewels couldn't tell the court about Wade, she had to once again get creative when asked how did Marcel take the fact that she wanted a divorce. She told them that he would come to the hotel everyday, and profess his love. She also told him that he made it clear that he would not allow the marriage to be over. But she never, ever, mentioned anything about Wade Wallace.

Mrs. Madison, are you an alcoholic?" the prosecutor asked her, continuing his grilling.

"Am I an alcoholic?" she laughed, trying to undermine the question. "That doesn't even sound right."

"The question is quite simple, are you or are you not an alcoholic?"

"If you're asking have I had a drink or two, then the answer would be of course. I am of age you know?"

"Do you abuse alcohol?"

"No, I certainly don't abuse alcohol."

"So even though, to hear you tell the court, you were in a volatile relationship, you would still have us to believe that you never, ever, tripped up and abused alcohol?"

Jewels held her head up high, looked at him, and then the courtroom and said, "Never. I was very responsible when it came to drinking."

● ● ●
The Truth:

Jewels was walking around Marcel's mansion with a bottle of wine in one hand, and a bottle of vodka in the other. She'd been drinking like this for weeks. She was cursing the day she ever met Marcel out loud, despite the fact that he wasn't home.

"You, dirty, dick, ugly mothafucka! I hate you! I fucking hate your guts." She splashed wine in her mouth, and washed it back with a gulp of liquor. Her wet lips sparkled under the chandelier's glow, and saliva and liquor flowed from the corners of her mouth. "You should've left us alone! You should've let us be!"

Why couldn't he leave her alone, was the question she asked herself over and over again. Why couldn't Marcel just let her have Wade? He had the world. He fucked four to five bitches in their bed at least twice a week, so it wasn't like he wasn't doing his thing. He even openly slept with his best friend Gia, despite giving her the tag *best friend*. He did it all. So what was he doing bothering her?

Wade was perfect. He was from her country. He worshipped the ground she walked on, and he wanted her and only her. And now he was gone. The beautiful man she adored was dead!

By the time Marcel walked into the house, Jewels was all the way turnt up. She was swaying from left to right, but the bottles of liquor were steady in her hand. "You look a fucking mess," he said walking past her and toward their room. "You need to sit your ass down somewhere, Jewels."

She followed him and said, "Ain't that something. If...if I looked...so fucked up, why you want me back? Huh?"—She burped—"why not just leave me the fuck alone?"— She burped louder— "Why take me from Wade?"

Marcel removed his watch and placed it in the watchcase on his dresser. "If you mention his name again, Jewels," he said calmly, "I'm going to smash your face toward the back of your scalp. The only reason I'm giving you a break is because you drunk. But I'm about to not give a fuck."

"Oh, so now you want to smash my face in"—she gulped the vodka—"isn't that special."

He turned around, leaned against the dresser and looked at her. "It's funny how you so mad at me right now, when you should be happy that somebody wants to still be bothered with you. You need to be on your knees."

"Nigga, I don't give a fuck about you wanting to be bothered with me! I was loved, I was fucking loved, and you took it from me."—She threw the bottle of wine at his head. It missed and it crashed against the wall, turning it light burgundy— "I fucking hate you! Do you hear me? I fucking hate you!"

He rushed up to her like he was preparing to knock her over. The first thing he did was snatch the bottle of vodka out of her hand, and slam it down on the dresser. And then he grabbed her face and licked it from the bottom of her chin, to the top of her nose. She could smell his stinky spit in one nostril. The he hugged her so tightly, she almost couldn't breathe. "I want to kill you so badly right now, Jewels, please don't make me. Please don't make me murder you."

Her nose was pressed into his chest, but still she was able to say, "I hate you so fucking much. I want you to kill me. Please kill me." She spoke directly into his heart so that he would feel she was serious.

He pushed her back, but maintained control of her shoulders. "Why so you can be with that nigga in hell? Naw, I'm not sending you to him just yet."

"You never loved me," she said hunching her shoulders forward. "You never even liked me."

"Jewels, I do love you, but you pushing your luck with me." His fingers were buried into the flesh of her arm. "I'm trying not to do the things to you that I know I can. I'm trying real hard. Now you know you had no business fucking with that dude, behind my back. It was foul of you to fuck my friend, and the sooner you understand it the better."

Although she was busted, she couldn't believe that he even fixed his lips to say something about sleeping with his friend. Wade never fucked with him the way she fucked with Bet. But fuck Bet, all she cared about was Wade. So he was the one that violated friends.

"You should've left me alone," she sobbed. "You should've let me be, Marcel."

"I couldn't do that," he walked away.

"But why, Marcel?" she followed him but kept her distance. "It's clear you hate me? Why couldn't you leave us alone, so that you could fuck Gia, Nia and the Santa Maria bitches?"

"Because you my wife, and the only reason that nigga was with you, was to taunt me. Don't you see it, baby?"— He pointed at his face— "Use your fucking eyes, and you'll see better! He wanted to take my wife, just because—"

"Just because what?" she interrupted. "Huh? The man didn't need your money."

"Just because you were mine. And make no mistake," he chuckled, removing his shoes. "If you believe he didn't want my money you are really fooled."

"I could see the love he had for me in his eyes." She said softly. "That man adored every part of me." Her voice was reduced to a whisper. "And I will never, *ever* forget him for as long as I live."

"You really do wanna die don't you? Huh? That's what you want to do?"

"Marcel, I don't care anymore."

"Well you should, if you really knew me, you would care." He pointed at her. "Because I wouldn't just kill you. Naw, that would be too simple. I would put you through the worst pain imaginable. I'm talking pure torture, baby."

"I loved Wade, and I will always love Wade."

Marcel took three quick breaths and rushed over to her. He grabbed her by the collar, and punched her in the center of the face, on the soft part between her nose and lips. She dropped to the floor and he climbed on top of her, like a monkey. Grabbing her by the shirt again, he punched her six more times, until his wrist ached. Her nose flattened, and blood filled to high levels in her mouth.

"I told you not to fuck with me didn't I?"—He punched her in the eye—"but you wouldn't listen! Why wouldn't you listen?"

Even if Jewels wanted to talk at this moment she couldn't. He was punishing her so severely that she was delirious. She thought she was back home in San Pedro Sula, Honduras, instead of America. She saw her mother's face, and smelled the mustiness of her underarms, as she gripped her into a loving hug. This life was a mess, and Jewels was okay with it being over.

"You so stupid, Jewels!" he released her shirt, and her head bounced on the carpet. "So fucking stupid."

He stood up and paced her body like a shark, trying to figure out what he could do with her next. How he could devour the parts of her that Wade touched, and leave everything else.

"I didn't want to do this to you," he said as he stooped down over her bludgeoned body and talked above her head. "I didn't want to hurt you. You should've never got up with Wade, baby. That nigga didn't love you. He wasn't going to take care of you like I did." He put his hand over his thumping heart. "You should've stayed away from him, Jewels. I mean, didn't you see what he was trying to do to us? Huh?" he looked down at her and saw her shallow breaths. "I know you don't understand this, but you needed this beating, because I never gave you one like this before. But ask Bet about me. I had her jaw wired twice and had her eating out of a tube for six months for less! So this is nothing, Jewels. I let you off easy. I didn't want you to see this part of me. I didn't want you to see it." He looked deranged and with her impaired vision, she didn't recognize him. "Do you know how many bitches I killed? Huh? Do you know how many I buried? Hundreds!" he said flashing a wide crazed smile. "You needed to see that I wasn't playing. You needed to see that I'm the one who owns you, not the other way around. I hope you understand now, Jewels."

He stood up and kicked her so many times, her insides shifted.

CHAPTER 19

In The Courtroom:

"So you claim that you are not an alcoholic, but isn't it true that you were admitted into a hospital for driving drunk?" the prosecutor questioned.

"No that's not true," she said, shaking her head briskly from left to right.

"What do you mean?"

"I did not get into a car accident."

"Are you sure about that?" he flipped a few sheets of paper in his hand, before stopping on one. "Because this police report indicates that you were driving while under the influence and crashed your car." He handed it to her, allowing her to look at the document.

"Well the police report lied, you fat mothafucka," she yelled, tossing the document to the floor.

She was sick of his fat, funky, dirty ass! She contemplated flying over the stand, and digging his eyes out.

The courtroom gasped when they heard her response, and Jewels knew she fucked up. She needed to keep her composure at all times, and instead she was becoming unraveled. When she looked at her attorneys, she saw disappointment all over their faces. Thanks to Jewels' outburst, she was giving the prosecution the ammunition they needed to win.

"One more outburst like that in my courtroom and you will be penalized severely," the judge warned. "Do you understand me, Mrs. Madison?"

Jewels looked up at the judge. "Yes, your honor, I do understand," she said softly, appearing meek again.

"I'll repeat the question."

The prosecutor picked the document up off of the floor, and tried to hide the smile on his face. *Yeah, keep doing dumb shit like that and you'll win the case for me.*

"The police report indicated that you crashed into a light post while under the influence of alcohol. As a result your face was bashed in, and both of your eyes were blackened. Is this true?"

"No, it isn't. It didn't happen in that way."

"Then explain."

"Marcel beat me to a pulp on the middle of my floor because I left him," she said. Although she was partially correct, she didn't say that he also beat her for being with Wade Wallace. "He also beat me because I filed for divorce. When I was about to die, he put me in my car, threw my car into drive and watched it roll into a light post. I had been drinking at home before he beat me, that's why they found the alcohol in my system."

"Even if what you say is true, then it must also be true that Marcel didn't want you to die."

"Marcel wanted to control me. He always wanted to control me. So he even wanted to control whether I lived or died."

*****

The Truth:

Marcel was on cloud nine. Earlier that day, he pulled off yet another successful heist at a dealership with his gang, and he got away with over three hundred thousand dollars. At this point in the game he didn't need to do these things, because his narcotics operation was more profitable and less risky. But Marcel got off on the robberies. Although he was good, as far as money was concerned, he sincerely missed the connection he had with his wife.

In a half assed attempt to make up for the beating, he had two pair of Christian Louboutins shoes in the backseat of his car, along with her new Louis Vuitton purse. Knowing how much she loved the labels, he was certain this would put him back into her good graces.

When he beat her the way that he did, staged her car accident and called 9-1-1 anonymously to report a car accident, he was happy when he learned she survived. He didn't want to kill her, just punish her for her wrongdoings. In the hopes that she could see the errors of her ways.

While she was in the hospital recuperating, he saw to it that all of her needs were cared for. He made sure that she had everything she needed, and spared no expense on his lovely wife.

Through everything he'd done for her, when he got her home, there was still a deep darkness behind her eyes. All she did was lie in the bed and stare out of the window, never using the rest of the house for anything. And when he tried to talk to her, she would turn her head and close her eyes.

She'd been home for two weeks, and her mood had not changed. In her sleep she called Wade's name, and Marcel had to prevent himself from killing her more than once for the unconscious disrespect.

When he called the house from North Carolina two days ago, she didn't answer the phone. He didn't have to wonder if she was still home or not, because he made Gia watch the house from a far. Gia confirmed that although Jewels was not answering, she had not left, and she wasn't happy about it either.

Walking through his front door, carrying the gifts in his hand, he wore a smile on his face until he was smacked in the middle of the head with a cast iron pan. The bags dropped out of his hands, and Marcel tumbled to the floor.

On a rampage, she banged him in the middle of his head five more times, and blood gushed out of his open wounds, and poured into his eyes. Jewels could care less about his feelings. She wanted him in agony.

She closed and locked the door. Filled with rage, she tapped into her female strength that was reserved for women who needed to lift cars off of their babies, and dragged his ass into the bathroom. She climbed into the tub, and pulled him inside with her. When she was done, she turned the shower on. The chilly water poured over her back, dampened her hair and made her look like a lunatic caught in the rain.

"You should've killed me mothafucka!" She screamed. "You should've fucking killed me!"

She hit him in the face once more for good measure, and then threw a towel over his face. She then allowed the water to run over the towel, thereby pausing his breathing mechanisms. Marcel felt paralyzed.

He choked, gasped for air, and tried to get up, only to be met with another blow to the face.

"You killed my true love, you dumb"—blow to the face—"piece"—blow to the face—"of shit!"

She turned the water off, yanked the towel off of his face and hit him again. That one was for free.

"You fucked with the wrong bitch," she pointed her finger in his nostril, "and you're going to see what kind of person I can be." She hit him in the face again.

While he was in the tub babbling, she grabbed a saline enema from under the sink. She sat on the toilet, removed the enema from the box and pushed it into her asshole. "You gotta understand, Marcel, I'm not a pushover"— she squeezed all of the saline into her body and threw the empty bottle on the floor— "I'm not someone you can take advantage of." She was allowing the enema time to work through her system. "I never told you about my life, mainly because you didn't ask. You didn't care!" she wiped the tears away from her eyes. "But I'm from Honduras"— she hit her chest hard— "San Pedro Sula, bitch! Your perfect country has nothing on mine! Comemos personas como tú en mi país!" she laughed.

In Spanish she said, "We eat people like you in my country!"

When she was done on the toilet, she climbed in the tub and positioned her ass over his face. Then she shit all over him. The wet dump landed in his eyes, mouth, nose and ears. When he coughed to catch his breath shit got into his throat too.

When she was done humiliating him, she smacked him in the head again with the cast iron pan and he passed out cold.

CHAPTER 20

In The Courtroom:

"So let me get this straight, you would like us to believe that you are not an alcoholic, despite the evidence? And that your husband beat you while you were drinking and staged a fake accident?"

"Yes, because as we all know, things are never as they seem," Jewels said confidently.

"Is that right," he said sarcastically. "If this is true, then we are also to believe that the same applies to you, and that we can't believe everything you say."

"No, that's not true. I'm being honest, because I'm sworn under oath." She leaned in. "He tried to kill me, and he must've felt bad and staged that scene. But I'm not an alcoholic."

"Speaking of trying to kill you, isn't it also true that before Mr. Madison was murdered, that you fired at him in your home?"

"That's not true!"

"Then how do you explain the gun fire in your home? Laurie Dickenson, another next door neighbor, reported to the investigators before Mr. Madison's murder that she heard gunfire at your residence."

"The gun went off by mistake," she lied. "But I wasn't the one holding it. That's all I can say."

"Well unfortunately for you, that's not going to be good enough."

● ● ●

The Truth:

When Marcel woke up the next day, his right wrist was handcuffed to his right ankle, and his left ankle was handcuffed to his left wrist. He looked like a weird crab sat up straight. He tried to wiggle out of the bind, but couldn't move. The cuffs were on tightly. The dried crust from Jewels' feces rested all over his hair, face and clothes, and he smelled the foul odor every time he breathed in. He could also feel the knots on his forehead pulsating from the cast iron blows to the face.

When Jewels opened the bathroom door, wearing nothing but the new black Christian Louboutins he bought her, he frowned.

"Wow, you really do know how to pick beautiful shoes. Thanks, Marcel." She stood in the middle of the door, placed her hands on the doorframe and raised her leg. This move also exposed the redness of her vagina. She wiggled her foot. "I absolutely love them."

Marcel frowned and asked, "So what are you going to do now? Fuck me?"

"Of course not, sweetie." She put her foot down. "I will never fuck you again in this lifetime. Didn't you get the memo?" she rubbed her hand between her legs. "This pussy belongs to the late great Wade Wallace."

He sighed. "Jewels..."

"Juliette, my baby prefers me to be called Juliette. He refused to buy into the nickname you gave me, and you know what, I have to respect his request."

"Juliette, what are you going to do with me now?"

She walked further into the bathroom. "It depends." She shrugged. "Because the thing is, I can do so much to you. Don't you see, Marcel, this is your payback? I mean, everybody has to get paid back in life. Wade's death was my payback, because I didn't leave with him the moment I saw his face, because I knew he was the one. And your payback is the extreme torture I have planned for what you did to him."

"What are you going to do with me?" he said, angrily. His dick was hard because he wanted to strangle her so badly.

"It depends," she said.

When he looked at the inside of her thighs, and saw blood running down her legs he said, "You do know that you on your period right?"

"Of course I do," she giggled. She squatted, stuffed a finger into her pussy, and smeared her blood inside his nostril, and upper lip. When she stuffed a finger inside of her pussy again, and felt a blood clot the size of a large grape, she pulled it out and forcefully stuffed it into his mouth.

"You dirty bitch!" he yelled spitting it to the floor.

She laughed hysterically. "It's just a little blood, mixed in with me and Wade's baby that you killed because you stressed me out." Her face was now serious. "You deserve to eat that shit."

He tried to hide his anger at learning that she was pregnant with Wade's child. It wasn't important anyway at the moment. His life was. "Can you please tell me what you're going to do with me now, Juliette? Please!"

"Well, my love, first I'm going to go into the kitchen and make me something to eat." She walked around him like a shark. In the same way he did her. "I'm thinking a big fat juicy steak. I'll probably cook some rice, and pour me a large glass of wine." The sounds of her high heels clicking scared him to death. He farted.

"Jewels, what are you—,"

"And then I'm going to take me a long bath," she interrupted him. She stopped in front of him, bent over in his face, and rubbed her bloody ass cheeks all over his nose.

"Move, bitch," he yelled into the flesh of her ass. He knew she was doing that raunchy shit just because she knew how he felt about a stinky pussy.

When he bit her ass, in an effort to get her out of his face, she didn't even flinch. Instead she stood up and said, "After I have eaten, and of course bathed, I'm going to take a long nap. And you my friend, will be here for days, with nothing to eat or drink."

His heart beat rapidly with the news. She was planning to starve him to death. "Jewels, I'm still your husband. Don't do something you can't take back."

"For now," she said softly. "Let us not forget, that I have already put in the paperwork for a divorce."

"Jewels, if you want a divorce, you don't have to go through all of this. I'll sign the papers right now! Where are they?"

"I'm not worried about that anymore, sweetheart. I'm on some other shit right now." She walked toward the door. "Good night, my beloved." She closed it softly behind her.

Six Days Later

Jewels went about her life day after day, while her husband sat on the bathroom floor wasting away. She didn't have a penny's worth of remorse for him, because he deserved the torture. In her opinion he'd done everything he could to ruin her life, and because of it he had to pay. Only when she felt bad for him, would she un-cuff him and let him go. That's if that day ever came.

When she woke up on the sixth day, for some reason something felt different. She glanced at the clock and saw the time read 1:30 pm. And although the air conditioner wasn't on, and all of the windows were closed, a strange chill rolled over her body.

Slowly she got up, and walked to the bathroom on the lower level. The moment she bent the corner, her heart felt as if it stopped when she saw the bathroom door had been kicked out.

"Oh my, God, no," she yelled covering her mouth with both hands. "He didn't get away, please God, don't let him have gotten away."

When she looked at the bathroom floor, she saw piss puddles, shit stains and the handcuffs sitting on the middle of the floor. She didn't know that because Marcel was starved that he was able to ease out of the cuffs with no problem.

Jewels rushed back to her room, unlocked the safe under the bed, and removed her .45 handgun. With it firmly in her hands, she checked the entire house for his whereabouts.

"If you are in here, Marcel, I'm going to fucking kill you," she yelled looking around carefully. "I'm not playing with you! Plus Wade's people are asking about him. They are going to come looking for you."

She went through the entire house and didn't find him anywhere.

After two weeks passed, she realized he wasn't coming home due to Wade's people. *Maybe they killed him already.* She thought. She got comfortable, especially when she changed the code to the alarm system and re-keyed all of the doors. In her mind he must have realized how crazy she could be, and left her alone.

She just stepped out of the shower when she opened the bathroom door, only to see her husband looking better than ever. The weight he lost did him well, and made him look even younger.

"Hello, Jewels," he smiled. "It's good to see you again."

She grabbed the towel and covered her body. She slowly backed up toward the toilet. "How did you get in here? I changed the locks, and the code."

"Yep, and I paid the same people you used to set everything up." He strolled slowly toward her.

"Marcel, I've been thinking about what I did to you, and I know it was wrong," she said honestly. "But...but you did me so bad that I wanted you to pay."

"I know, Jewels," he said, rushing toward her.

The moment he did, he judged incorrectly, because Jewels grabbed the .45 off of the toilet, aimed and fired. The bullet pierced his flesh immediately.

Before Jewels shot him, he didn't think she had it in her.

CHAPTER 21

In The Courtroom:

"So after Marcel fired the gun by accident, was anybody hurt?" the prosecutor asked.

Juliette told the prosecutor that Marcel was cleaning his gun, and it went off, firing into the bedroom wall by mistake.

"No," she lied. "Nobody got hurt at all."

The Truth:

After she shot him, and blood gushed out of his hand, she immediately felt remorse. She was so devastated by her actions, that she dropped the gun and dashed over to help him. "Oh my, God, baby, I'm so sorry," she wept. "I can't believe I did this shit. I can't believe I shot you!" She grabbed a hand towel from the wall and wrapped his hand gently.

"I'm okay, baby, I'm fine," he said softly. "I just gotta get out of here and go get some help."

"I can't believe I did this," she sobbed harder. "I was so angry with you, Marcel. I was mad at everything and I lost my mind."

"I know, baby, and I came here to kill you tonight," he said trying to hide the pain in his face. "But, I can see now that you still love me, and it's not too late for our marriage. But I gotta go, baby, because I'm losing a lot of blood." He walked out of the bathroom, trailing blood throughout the house. "I gotta get this wound taken care of, before I die."

When he turned around she saw a huge hunting knife, and rope tucked in the back of his jeans. This horrified Jewels. She knew immediately that he wasn't just coming to murder her, but to activate extreme torture.

When he came back later that night, Jewels rushed up to him, and greeted him at the doorway. "Are you okay?" she looked at his bandaged hand.

He smiled. "Of course I'm fine. I'm a gangsta." He turned around and waived at Gia, who gave Jewels the evil eye before speeding off in her car.

Jewels could feel a ball of hate stirring up in her belly all over again, and it showed all over her face. Why hadn't he called her to pick him up if he couldn't drive? She was realizing the pain that women all over the world knew who were in broken marriages. And it was, whenever you make a decision that your marriage is over, and accept it in your heart, only to be pulled back in by your no good husband again, the pain will be ten times as worse. When Gia dropped him off it showed Jewels that he wasn't going to change. He was intent on trying to change her.

"She just can't stay away can she?" She walked away from him, and flopped down on the living room sofa.

He sat next to her. "She's my best friend, Jewels. What do you expect?"

She stood up and looked at him. He flinched a little, because the last time she was standing over top of him, she was starving him and rubbing her bloodied pussy all over his face. And at the moment, she looked just as angry.

"You can't have me, and her too, Marcel." She pointed at the window. "Don't you see the difference in me? I have changed and will never allow that again. Not at any cost."

He sighed. "Jewels, please lets not go through this again. Haven't we been through enough? You starved and beat—"

"You beat me first," she interrupted.

His head dropped. "I know and I'm sorry. You got me so confused. I just don't need this right now."

"Need what, Marcel? Me? Her? What exactly are you referring too? Or maybe it's the fact that I won't allow you to be around a woman who's clearly trying to take you away from me. Because if that's what you're asking me to do it is never happening again. Ever!"

"Baby, listen to me, Gia has saved my life way before you even entered the picture."

"Then why didn't you marry her," she asked sitting next to him again. "If you want to marry her you have my blessings, and I will let you go, Marcel." She placed her hand over her heart. "I thought I hated you, but I found out that I love you that much to remove my hands off of you. Is that what you want?"

"No, because I don't look at her like that."

She eased down, and sat at his feet. Looking up at him she said, "Marcel, I'm different now." She rubbed his knee softly. "I'm different in the way I move, think and feel. I know now that I deserve happiness and I want a chance to love you right. But if I give you my heart this time, and you break it, you must understand that it comes with a warning label."

"What you saying, Jewels?"

She sighed and looked down at the floor. "If she remains in your life"— she looked at him— "in any aspect whatsoever, then I won't. And if you stay with me, I will not play those games anymore. Someone will get hurt."

"So you're giving me an ultimatum?"

"If you want to call it that you can, but if you choose to look at it a different way you can say I'm giving us a fair chance to work out our marriage. I mean, don't you want that as much as I do?"

"You know I do."

"Well then what's the problem, Marcel? Why do I feel like I don't have your heart right now?"

"I ain't wit' how you making me choose." He stood up and walked away. "I mean, I love you, Jewels, I really do." He looked down at his bandaged hand. "But I've never had a woman treat me the way that you did."

"You mean you never had a woman fight back," she said confidently.

"Be careful," he warned.

"No, you be careful," she yelled. "Take a good look at me, Marcel, because for better or worse, I am going to make someone happy." She stood up and walked up to him. She grabbed his unwounded hand and looked up into his eyes. "I know I seem mad, but I will never disrespect you on purpose, I want you to be my king, Marcel. Despite everything that has happened, as of right now I'm still your wife. But things must change if it doesn't I'm going to take myself away from you."

He snatched his hand away and glared at her. "That's just it, you don't take anything from me!" he stomped, flopped on the couch and rubbed his head. This new and approved Juliette had him so confused. Had him ques-

tioning who was in charge. Even her walk was different.
"You tried to kill me."

"And you tried to kill me."

"But I didn't," Marcel yelled.

"And you still breathing too."

She walked up to him but remained standing. "So what do we do now?"

"I don't know, Jewels. I don't know."

"Maybe we should separate then," she replied. "If we do that maybe we'll be able to sort things out."

"Is that what you really want?"

"Yes, because I don't see any other way right now." She stood straight up and raised her head toward the sky. "I am Juliette Madison, born Alejandra Ramos, and I will not sit down lightly while you or anybody else hurts me again. The day of the suckers is over."

It was the first time he heard her original birth name, but it wouldn't be the last.

CHAPTER 22

In The Courtroom:

Jewels told the prosecutor how she and Marcel tried to work on their marriage, despite the problems.

"So when you decided to work on your marriage, was it an honest attempt on your part?" he asked.

"Yes, like I said, I really wanted my marriage to work." She placed her hand over her breasts. "From the bottom of my heart I did, because I loved Marcel."

"So how did things turn out?"

"Weird," she said clearing her throat. "I didn't know how much I changed, after I first left him. How my thoughts changed. I started to realize that I felt I needed Marcel, because I didn't deserve anyone better."

"Why do you say that?"

Jewels remained silent, as big globs of tears poured down her face. They were the kind of tears that came from the soul.

"Because I cursed my mother."

"Cursed your mother for what?"

Juliette thought back to when she was taken from her country in a suitcase, and thrown on a plane like dirty luggage. That period in her life was frightening, and extremely painful. Her body being placed in the awkward position, and shaken around in the bottom of the airplane caused her to vomit, and was extremely traumatic for her. The entire time Jewels was angry and begged God to kill her mother for causing her so much grief. For five hours she begged God to make her mother feel just one inch of the amount of pain she felt. It was a repeated prayer. And she got her wish too, when Kathia Ramos stepped in front of a moving bus, just so that she wouldn't be a burden on her daughter.

Jewels never forgave herself for her mother's suicide, and believed she was the cause of her death, because she asked for it. So she allowed Marcel to abuse her both mentally and physically, and even sabotaged the love that Garrick and Wade tried to give her. In court was the first time she admitted it to herself silently.

"I cursed my mother for leaving me," she said, wiping her tears away. She couldn't elaborate because to say more would implicate her, and shed light on the fact that she was not from this country.

"What happened with the separation?" The prosecutor saw the tears, and decided to take his questioning another route, in case the jury started feeling sympathy for her.

"Well, after we separated, I grew comfortable being alone." She wiped more tears away with the back of her hand. "After awhile I discovered that I didn't need him anymore to make me feel good about myself. I was good with being alone, which was the first time that ever happened in my life." She smiled into the courtroom, looking at no one in particular. "When he left for those four weeks, I was forever changed," she said truthfully.

The Truth:

It had been to weeks since Jewels had seen Marcel. Since they were separated, she decided to work on herself. She made a decision that she would no longer be manipulated by anybody, not even by her husband. Finally her feelings were first and everybody else's was second, if at all.

Marcel called everyday asking her if he could come home, and each day she told him no, and that she needed more time. At first she thought the reason she couldn't be with him anymore was because of Gia. But after awhile she realized what she always knew. That Wade exposed her to true love, and it was time to move on.

Jewels had just come home from college, when she opened the door to see Marcel in the kitchen preparing dinner.

"Come here, baby," he smiled waving her over. "I'm making fried chicken, green beans and jasmine rice. You know you could never fuck with my fried chicken when I set my mind to it."

"I hate fried chicken remember?" she reminded him. "You once bought me a fried chicken sandwich, and I got thrown out your car for not eating it."

He felt stupid. "Yeah, well, fuck all of that shit," he said disregarding her comment, and her feelings. "You can just eat beans and rice."

She threw her purse on the kitchen counter. "What are you doing here, Marcel? I mean, I thought we were separated."

"How long did you actually think that would last?" he asked flipping over the chicken. "It ain't like I didn't buy this fly ass crib. Why should you be the only one to enjoy it?

"Marcel, but we agreed," she yelled. "Baby, I need more time to get my mind straight."

Really she needed more time to find another place to live. She thought about calling Garrick, but decided not to use him anymore. He didn't deserve that pain, and she finally understood how it felt. She needed to stand on her own two feet.

"It ain't rocket science, Jewels, either you love me or not. Besides, I told Gia today that I can't be her friend no more, Jewels. You got your wish already, okay? So relax."

Although Jewels' body tingled due to what she imagined her face looking like when he told her the news, because she hated Gia so much, she knew that wasn't good enough anymore. As far as she was concerned he should've come to that conclusion years ago, so what took him so long?

"I hope you didn't do that for me, Marcel."

"No I didn't," he said lifting the lids to one of the pots and stirring the green beans. "I did it for us." He put the lid back on and turned around to look at her.

"But I don't want you to do it for us anymore."

His eyebrows rose. "Jewels, do you still want a divorce?"

"I didn't say that," she sighed sitting down. Of course she wanted a divorce but the look he gave her said he wouldn't be able to take the rejection.

"Then what do you want," he yelled. When she jumped he reduced the base in his voice. "Baby, we've been through everything together." He approached her and grabbed her hand. "I beat you, you starved and shot me and we still here."

"That's not romantic, Marcel," she said. "That's dysfunctional."

"Why it gotta be dysfunctional? Our life doesn't have to be like everybody else's for it to work. I mean look at how we got married. Don't you remember when I proposed to you?"

She looked at the marble on the counter. "It seems like a long time ago but yes, it was during 9/11."

"I never told you this, but before I saw your face in that airport I had all intentions of taking my own life if you were on that plane. I fucking love you, Jewels. You my world. And yes, I made a few moves that weren't right, but I understand now what it means to be married. I'm ready baby."

She pulled her hands out of his. "I can't do this anymore," she said softly, looking down at her feet. "I can't be with you." She looked into his eyes.

"Just give me one more chance, Jewels." He massaged her shoulders a little to roughly. "If I even think about fucking up again, you can cut me off."

"Marcel, I don't know," she said under her breath. "I have a feeling if we stay together, somebody will die."

"And I don't care just as long as you die with me," he said. "Stay with me," Jewels"— He kissed her on the lips— "Stay with me, baby. Don't give up on me now. Don't give up on us."

"It's over," she said softly.

Marcel's fingers gently stroked her beautiful face. "Say yes that you'll stay with me. I'm dying, baby."

He trailed kisses along the side of her neck, before licking her earlobe softly. After wetting her ear a little, he nibbled on it a little hard, which caused Jewels' pussy to tingle. It was her hot spot.

"Say yes, baby," he whispered again. "I can feel your body heating up. You still love me even though it's been months since I touched you."

He slowly unfastened her shirt, revealing her perky breasts. When her top was off, he removed his shirt. She reveled at the hardness of his chest, and the perfectness of his features. Marcel Madison, even now, was one of the most beautiful men she'd ever seen before in her life. From his golden hair, to his bronzed skin, he was flawless. But it was his heart that was detestable.

With a look of lust in his eyes, he clutched her neck and squeezed lightly. She knew that at the moment, her life was in his hands, but she wasn't afraid. Fear never did anything to help her before anyway, so she was not going to give into it anymore.

"Say yes," he said again, kissing her chin. He squeezed her throat tighter, forcing a few breaths from her lungs.

Instead of telling him to stop, she made her peace with God, and told Wade and her mother that she was on her way.

"I am Alejandra Ramos, and I will never love you again."

She turned her eyes away, as a tear rolled down her cheek. But instead of killing her, he kissed her passionately while removing her pants. When she was naked, he stuffed his finger into her tight pussy and fingered her roughly. Her pussy heated up like an oven and got wetter. It was true that he had her body, but he didn't have her heart.

"Say yes," he demanded.

When she didn't respond, he turned her around and bent her over on the counter like a cheap whore. Her pink pussy opened for him, and he stuffed his dick into her roughly.

"You are mine, Jewels Madison. I don't know who this Alejandra person you keep talking about is, but I will never let you go."

And for that you must die. She thought.

CHAPTER 23

In The Courtroom:

"So you said that you tried to reconcile with your husband, Mrs. Madison, but you don't sound too sure. So my next question is, did it work?"

She shifted in her seat and under her breath said, "I...kind...uh..."

"I'm sorry, Mrs. Madison. We could not hear you, did the reconciliation work or not," he raised his voice. "We need you to speak louder for the court."

"It didn't work, but I really wanted it to."

"Explain to the court your account the day Marcel was murdered."

● ● ●

The <u>Lie</u> She Told The Court

Jewels was walking around like a zombie in her own home when Marcel walked in the front door with a huge grin on his face. "Baby, I have an idea, lets go on a picnic today."

She sat on the sofa and looked up at him. His presence irritated her so much, that when she saw him she immediately felt drained. "I don't know about that, Marcel. I'm kind of tired and all I really want to do is get into bed, and close my eyes."

"You've been sleeping all day, Jewels," he said rubbing her shoulders. "Come on, baby. Come with me. I have the whole day planned out for us and it'll be nice."

She looked up into her husband's eyes. "This would really mean a lot to you wouldn't it?"

"It would mean everything to me."

"Then I'll go."

Marcel was extra excited as they piled into his car. When they made it to a secluded park, in Virginia, over thirty miles away from any homes or gas stations, she felt a little awkward. Something didn't feel right in her spirit. But Marcel had placed so much effort into the picnic, and the day was so beautiful, that she decided to give him a chance.

After sitting on the red plaid blanket, she watched as Marcel unloaded the beautiful wooden and red basket. First he removed a bottle of red wine, and then some cheese, crackers and grapes. He poured a glass of wine for her and then himself.

"To us," he said as he made a toast.

She softly clinked her glass against his and said, "To us."

"You know I love you right," he said eyeing her. "And I will always love you."

She took a sip of her wine. "I know, Marcel, and at first I was feeling like this might not work out, but now that I think about it, I'm really willing to give us a chance."

"Good, I'm glad you feel that way, because I want to talk to you about some things."

"What about?"

"Well, Jewels, I understand that you don't like Gia, but her brother recently contacted me, and said that she was taken to a hospital, because of how I treated her.

Said she feels like I abandoned her for no reason. I haven't spoken to her in three weeks, Jewels, and I feel bad about it."

Jewels downed all of her wine. "Why is it that Gia must always be a topic of discussion with us?"

"Because she was in my life before you."

"And I'm in your life now, Marcel. And I don't feel comfortable with you bringing someone else into the picture anymore that you fucked. Don't you understand?"

"I understand that you keep giving me ultimatums. I understand that I would never tell you who to befriend. And I understand that I'm the husband and you're the wife, and that you have to trust me."

"I don't have any more friends remember? You fucked the only friend I've ever had in my life, and you made it clear where your heart lies. With Gia." She sighed. "You have such a double standard when it comes to your marriage, Marcel. I mean it's okay for you to do whatever you want, but not me. I was loved by someone and because of your jealousy, you took Wade away from me and that was unfair. I loved him!"

"I told you about bringing up Wade's name didn't I? Didn't I tell you about that shit?" He stood up and punched Jewels in the face.

● ● ●

In The Courtroom:

"Who is Wade?" the prosecutor asked her. "Throughout your entire testimony"— he flipped a few pages over on the clipboard— "you have never mentioned Wade's name. Who is he?"

"He was...uh...he was the one person...that cause I was...and," Jewels became totally unraveled.

Her face was a fresh, shiny mess due to sweating so much. She had been doing so well with lying all day, and now she fucked up in monumental like proportions. Not only did she mention another man, she mentioned her love for him.

"Your honor, may I have a moment to confer with my client?" Adele yelled popping up.

"No you may not, and the defendant will answer the question."

Adele took a seat and looked at her client.

"Who is Wade?" the prosecution asked.

Jewels looked at her attorney, hoping she could do something to help her. Because she knew in the back of her mind, just with the mentioning of his name, the prosecution would dig deep into her past and find out about him. Would they also discover that he was dead?

"He was, he was the love of my life."

The courtroom gasped.

"Well where is he now?"

"Only Marcel knows."

CHAPTER 24

In The Courtroom:

"So now we have learned that this Wade person was the man who actually had your heart," the prosecutor said, trying desperately to keep the smile off of his face. "And since you've given endless testimony of always being faithful, please tell the court why we should believe anything else that you have said thus far?"

Jewels sobbed and wiped her tears with the tissue in her hand. "Because Marcel was really an awful man. Who didn't want anybody to be happy! All I wanted to do is be happy. I tried to leave the marriage, but he wouldn't let me!"

"But you've told us that you were trying to reconcile with your husband. If this is the case, where is this Wade person now?"

"Like I said, only Marcel knows, when he told him to stay out of our lives, I didn't see Wade again after that. But I heard that he may have possibly moved out of state."

Jewels hated lying for Marcel, but what could she do? Say he was dead and that she knew about it, and didn't say anything to the authorities? She had enough shit to eat on her plate as it was. She didn't need anymore or anybody else's.

"How convenient that this Wade person is out of state."

"It's all true," she said. "And I know I had Wade in my life, but I truly loved my husband at one point and time, I was just tired of the hurt and the pain."

"If you loved your husband, and you really wanted things to work out, can you please tell the court why Marcel Madison is no longer with us?"

What Really Happened:

Jewels was walking around in the house like a zombie when Marcel walked in the front door with a huge grin on his face. She made a decision on where she was going to live and she hated it. But, she was sure she'd be able to get on her feet, and would never have to live in such squalor again if her plan worked out right.

"Baby, I have an idea, lets go on a picnic," Marcel said clapping his hands like a little bitch. He walked up to Juliette who was sitting on the sofa.

"Marcel, I ain't going to no fucking picnic with you! I'm sick of all of this fake ass shit around here. We fucked the one time in the kitchen, and now you automatically think shit is sweet between us, when in actuality I don't want to be bothered with you anymore. I mean let's keep shit real, Marcel. I know you're fucking with Gia again, and I warned you about trying to play me, but you didn't listen."

"Baby, I'm not fucking with her anymore," he said rubbing her shoulders. "You gotta believe me. Now please come with me. I want to do something special for you." Juliette rolled her eyes. "Please, Jewels, I have everything planned for us today and I promise it'll be nice."

She looked into his eyes. "I said I'm not going nowhere with you. Kick carpet, nigga."

Suddenly he grew angry. "Either you come with me or you can get the fuck out of my house, today. And since I already know you're making plans to leave this is going to be a huge inconvenience for you if you got to get the fuck out now."

How did he know? She thought.

"Now what you wanna do?" he asked.

She shook her head in frustration. "Well I guess I don't have any choice now do I?" she snatched her purse off of the sofa and followed him out of the door.

When they made it to a secluded park in Virginia, over thirty miles away from other homes or a gas station, Jewels felt a little awkward. Something was terribly off, and a small voice in her head told her to go.

After sitting on the red plaid blanket, she watched as Marcel unloaded the beautiful wooden and red picnic basket. First he removed a bottle of red wine which she was sure was poisoned, and then some cheese, crackers and grapes. With everything out of the bag he poured her a glass of wine and then himself.

"To us," he said raising his glass. He took a sip so she knew it was fine.

"Go fuck yourself, Marcel," She said not accepting his cheers.

"You know I love you right," he said putting his glass down. "And I will always love you."

She took a sip of her wine. "Nigga, when are you going to get to the purpose of this shit?" she looked around. "Because if you ask me, this entire set up is rather gay, and unlike you. I don't have time for the bullshit with you anymore, Marcel. Let's get to the point."

"You know what, you are one selfish ass bitch." He frowned and she could see his eye twitching as he looked at her. "It's my fault, because I spoiled you, but I would've never known that you would've turned out so badly."

"Tell me something you haven't told me already," Juliette responded.

"Why you hate me so much?"

"I don't have my list with me, since you pulled me out of the house," she said sarcastically, "but for starters you ruined my life, took Wade from me, gave me a sexually transmitted disease, and almost tried to beat me to death before you changed your mind and tried to cover it up with a fake ass car accident. And then you have the nerve to want me to accept the outsiders."

"By outsiders are you talking about Gia?"

Jewels finished her glass and poured herself some more. "What you think?"

"Well, Jewels, I think it's mighty funny how you can talk about Gia, when you gave that nigga some pussy. If anything you were just as guilty as I was. And then got the nerve to want somebody to feel sorry for you. Well I'm not feeling sorry for you anymore, Jewels. I've made a decision to be with her, and I brought you here to let you down easy."

Instead of being angry Jewels broke out into hysterical laughter. She absolutely could care less. "You are so fucking arrogant and cocky," she wiped the funny tears from her face. "You so caught up into your own world, that you not even listening when a bitch tells you that she doesn't give a fuck anymore. Go do you, boo, because

197

I'm done." She stood up and brushed the back of her jeans off. "Get up and take me home, nigga."

Marcel's blood was raging. Before now, he never had a woman not care if he left or stayed. He was embarrassed and more than anything his feelings were hurt. There were many things Jewels didn't know about her poor husband. In anger he told her he was a murderer the last time he beat her, but she had forgotten all about it. In actuality he killed many. Marcel didn't do well with rejection from women, which was why he surrounded himself with so many. So the way that Jewels was speaking to him was not only a blow to the ego, but causing him extreme mental anguish.

Angry, and without another word, he stood up and stole her in the face like a nigga in a boxing ring. Caught off guard, Jewels dropped to the grass, and he fell on top of her. He placed his hands around her neck, like he did the last time they had sex, but this time he squeezed tightly, and with a purpose. There would be no kissing on the earlobe, or whispers of sweet nothings this time. This was a first class attempt to take her life.

When she looked into Marcel's eyes, Jewels knew this was the moment she was going to die. It was obvious that in the moment he had lost all love for her. Sweat poured down off of his face, and dropped into her eyes, stinging and blinding her at the same time.

"You selfish, ass bitch! I made you," he said, veins popping up in the middle of his head as he continued to strangle her. "If it wasn't for me, you'd still be in a shelter, probably selling pussy for fifty cent a pop."

She placed her hand softly on his shoulder and whispered, "Marcel, please. You're killing me."

He was exhibiting no signs of letting up so she reached her hand out, and grabbed the knife that sat next to the cheese. When she had it in her hand, she stabbed him in the back once and then twice.

Immediately he fell off and she stabbed him again in the stomach. He was trying to get up, but she stabbed him again on the arm. Blood was over everything and everywhere. When he lay motionless in the grass, she ran down the hill, leading out of the park and into traffic. In her mind he was running behind her, and she needed help before he got his hands on her again.

Unfortunately for Jewels her night and shining armor would come in the form of a Virginia State Trooper. She was caught red-handed, literally, and dropped the bloody knife at her feet.

Jewels was arrested and taken in for questioning, but refused to tell them where Marcel's body was. Although she claimed self-defense, because she wouldn't give his whereabouts, she was detained. Marcel's body was eventually discovered the following morning, and Jewels was charged with First Degree Murder.

In The Courtroom:

"Are you going to answer the question or not Mrs. Madison? If you loved your husband, and you really wanted things to work out, why is Marcel Madison no longer with us?"

Jewels was tired of the fucking prosecutor. He didn't know shit about her or her life, yet he acted as if he did. *The nerve of this clown.* She thought. So she removed the innocent girl look she was doing for the jury from her face. She leaned back in the seat, crossed her piss-stained legs and looked at him directly in the eyes. She wanted him to know that every word she was about to utter was true.

"Mr. Madison is not here anymore because it was either him or me, and unfortunately for him, I won."

The prosecutor felt a chill roll down his spine. He looked at the jury and said, "Well ladies and gentlemen. There you have it. Introducing the real Mrs. Juliette Madison."

The courtroom gasped.

"I object," Adele yelled.

"No further questions," the prosecutor responded, walking away.

CHAPTER 25

In The Courtroom:

Before the next witness could take the stand it had to be cleaned with Pine Sol due to Jewels urinating in her seat earlier. Although she claimed it was sweat, the judge had seen enough defendants on the stand in his day to know what it really was.

When everything was clean, Adele called her next witness. She was a beautiful black woman, with a honey brown complexion, a long flowing weave, which was as gorgeous as Jewels' natural hair.

"Please state your first and last name for the court," Adele asked.

"My name is Rain Ayers," she said softly.

"Please spell your last name."

"Ayers," she repeated. "That's A...Y...E...R...S."

"Thank you."

Although Jewels had fucked shit up with her little performance earlier, Adele wasn't the best for no reason. She was determined to turn the situation around, and it started with Rain Ayers.

"Mrs. Ayers, how would you describe your relationship with Mr. Madison?"

"He was my fiancé," she said confidently.

The courtroom erupted in ooh's and ah's and the judge brought down his gavel with major force. "Order in the court! Order in my court!"

Everyone quickly settled down.

Based on the court and the jury's response, Adele was confident that this would work out in her client's favor. "Can you please repeat your answer for the record?"

"I said that Marcel Madison was my fiancé, for over ten years," she said, placing her long hair behind her ear.

"Did you know that he was already married?"

She held her head down and started sobbing. "No I didn't." she looked over at Jewels who wore an emotionless expression. "We have a little girl together and everything."

This caused Jewel's jaw to drop. Not only did he sleep around on her, he fucked around and got somebody pregnant. *You are such a dirty dog, Marcel! I hope you rot in hell.* She thought.

Adele pulled a sheet of paper from the file and said, "Your honor I would like to submit this DNA test taken by the *Office of Child Support Enforcement* to validate the witness's answer." She gave the judge and the prosecution a copy of the test. She focused back on the witness and said, "Where did you think he was staying at night when he wasn't with you?"

"I miss Marcel, I really do, but he was such a liar that it was hard to tell. I mean, he flat out told me that he was with his best friend Gia, who I couldn't stand. And now I discover that he was married. I'm devastated."

Although the prosecutor cross-examined Rain, he still wasn't able to make her look bad. Rain had proven to be a credible witness for the defense and it was on to Adele's next subject.

Kadee Wright was a tall beautiful woman, from Africa. Her defined bone structure and chocolate stunning features made her look more like a model, as she strutted through the courtroom. She was even able to rock her shiny baldhead, which surprisingly made her look just as feminine as Adele and Jewels with their luscious manes.

"Ms. Wright, what was your relationship with the defendant?" Adele asked, approaching the stand.

In a strong African accent she said, "I'm totally confused right now." Her voice was low and shaky. "I don't even believe what is going on. I don't understand why Marcel is dead."

Adele immediately grew worried. She was afraid she was about to back out on what she told them, thereby hurting her client's case even more. "Why do you say that?"

"Because Marcel was with me most nights. I mean, I never, ever would've expected that he was married. He stayed in my home at least three out of seven nights a week, unless I was in Africa. He put me up in my apartment and even had keys."

"When you say put you up, what do you mean?"

"He paid for everything, him and Gia both. As a matter of fact, we participated in a polyamory relationship, which I took very seriously. I dedicated my heart to both of them."

"Can you explain to the court what a polyamory relationship is?"

"Yes, of course." She cleared her throat. "The three of us, me, Marcel and Gia that is," she nodded, "were in a committed relationship. I loved them with all of my heart, and I thought they loved me back. They even gave me a bank account where they deposited money every week for me." She began to sob uncontrollably.

"Do you know where he got the money?"

"Yes, of course, he worked in construction." She sighed. "I'm confused...I'm so confused."

After Adele questioned the witness, it took a moment before she was calm enough for the prosecution to cross-examine her. But when he did, he knew that she was also a great witness for the defense, and there was nothing else he could do to change that.

Adele's next witness was Erika Seymour. She was a beautiful white woman with long flowing blonde hair and piercing blue eyes. By this time it was evident to everyone that Marcel knew how to pick them.

"Ms. Seymour, what was your relationship with Marcel Madison?"

"He was my boyfriend, and that bitch over there killed him," she yelled pointing at Jewels with a stiff finger.

"Order in the court," the judge said when everyone gasped. He then focused on Erika. "Another outburst like that and you will be in contempt. Now unless you want to spend a night in jail, you'd better be careful, young lady."

Erika told everybody at home how she was going to unleash on Jewels in court. And now that she did, and realized she was about to be locked up for acting a fool, she squeezed her ass cheeks together to prevent from farting due to being so scared. "I'm sorry your honor," she said. "I'll settle down."

Adele hid her displeasure with the witness to get back to business. "What was your relationship with Mr. Madison?"

"We were boyfriend and girlfriend," she sighed loudly. "At least that's what he told me."

"How long were you dating Mr. Madison?"

"For ten years, and everybody knows that he loved me very much. We went everywhere together, and went through everything."

"The defense would like to enter into evidence these pictures."

She handed the judge copies, and presented the prosecution with copies too. Adele already placed the pictures on a slideshow on the computer, to show the jury, which flashed on a screen. Picture after picture showcased Erika and Marcel living it up. In ninety percent of the photos he was kissing her, and it was evident that he was in a relationship with this woman. But it was the last picture that showcased the man Marcel really was.

"Erika, can you please tell the court how you got the black eye."

"Yes, sometimes I have a smart mouth, as you can clearly see." She looked up at the judge and smiled. "Anyway, Marcel decided to put me in my place. It wasn't a big deal; he did that all the time. If you ask me all women should be punished for disrespect and Marcel was good at it. He may have been violent, but he didn't deserve to be killed."

Adele, realizing she hit pay dirt with her, because she admitted that Marcel was a woman beater, looked at the prosecutor and said, "Your witness."

CHAPTER 26

In The Courtroom:

"...You have to understand, Marcel loved Jewels very much, and I was only in their relationship to make things better," Gia Apa told the prosecutor during questioning. "My presence was for both of them."

Gia had been going on and on since she'd been on the stand about the man Marcel was. To hear her tell it he was the second coming of Christ.

"Are you saying that Juliette Madison was a willing participant in the relationship you had with her husband?"

"Of course!" She looked at Juliette and licked her lips. "She told me she loved when I tasted her pussy, and couldn't get enough of me. Isn't that right, Jewels?" She grinned.

"That's a lie, you dirty bitch," Juliette yelled standing up. "I hated you! It's because of you Marcel is dead!"

The gavel came down so hard, the wood sounding block under it fractured. "Mrs. Madison you have been warned," the judge said pointing the gavel at her. "The next time you make an outburst like that in my court room you will be held in contempt. Am I clear?"

"Yes your honor"— she took her seat and scooted closer to the table— "I'm very sorry." She folded her hands on the table in front of her, and tried to appear harmless. It wasn't working, and Gia grinned, loving every minute of it.

"Like I was saying," Gia said rolling her eyes at Jewels. "She knew about our relationship, and was with it until Wade came into the picture. After her precious boyfriend got involved, she didn't want me around anymore and started causing problems between Marcel and me. It was only because she was doing her own dirt behind his back. The thing is, Marcel and I had been friends for years."

"Why do you say she was coming between you two?"

"Truthfully I believe that she was using me as a way to end her marriage. She already wanted to leave to be with the boy Wade. Actually who wouldn't want to be with him," she said crossing her legs, as she sat back in her chair. "The man is fine, and a good friend of mine."

"What kind of relationship would you say that Jewels and Marcel had?"

"I object," Adele said. "The witness is not a licensed doctor, and therefore can not give a professional opinion on the condition of my client's marriage."

"Your honor, I'm simply asking for the witness's personal opinion, since it has been proven by all, including Juliette, that Gia was involved in some capacity in their relationship."

"I'll allow it," the judge responded. "The witness may answer the question."

"Like I was saying," Gia said swinging her long luscious hair over her right shoulder. "Jewels was a very, very, angry person. And if you ask me it seemed like she was like that all of the time. Half of the time Marcel was on edge, and he was never himself after she came into the picture. He was totally miserable being married to her, but he tried to make it work. "

Jewels wasn't the only person that could lie in the courtroom, because Gia was also laying it on thick.

"In your earlier testimony, you told us that Mrs. Madison actually shot Marcel before. But we don't have any records of him going to the hospital on file. Or of him being shot."

"He went to a veterinarian," she said truthfully. "To protect her," she nodded at Jewels. "He didn't want her getting arrested."

"What is the name of the veterinarian?"

"Oh, I don't know I'm sorry," she said, refusing to put the veterinarian totally out there. "Marcel didn't tell me all of that."

She was hoping that the prosecution would just take her word for it. But, she certainly wasn't willing to go full snitch mode, realizing that she'd already broken the code just by being there, and saying anything at all.

The prosecutor didn't believe Gia didn't know anything else, but he didn't hammer her too hard. After all, it was his fault that he didn't do a better job of fact finding with her earlier.

"You also testified that after their wedding, Mrs. Madison threatened you, and told you she would kill you if you didn't leave her husband alone. What did you do?"

"Honestly I was scared for my life, and didn't do anything," she lied. She wasn't hardly scared, just irritated.

"The prosecution would like to enter into evidence, the voicemails from the defendant, which were placed on Gia's phone." When the evidence was accepted, the prosecutor hit play. And the moment he did, you could hear the hate flying from Jewels' voice.

Voicemail #1
"If you don't stay away from my husband, I'm going to stab you and him so many times, you won't be able to tell where your body ends and his begins."

Voicemail #2
"I'm going to slice out your heart, bitch, and slide in your blood. Stay the fuck away from my husband!

Voicemail #3
"I know my husband is with you, enjoy him while he's still alive."

When the prosecution was done playing the voicemails, all Adele could do was hold her head low. She did her best to cross-examine Gia, but she knew that the voicemails did more damage than what could be repaired for her client. Still, she wasn't the best for nothing and she had one last bullet in her chamber. And when it was time, she was going to pull the trigger.

CHAPTER 27

In The Courtroom:

Ansel Gord, from *My Life Insurance Agency* sat on the stand with his hands folded in front of him. The agent wrote the Madison's life insurance policy, and he had much to say on the matter of Marcel's death. First of all Jewels lied and claimed she didn't have an insurance policy on Marcel, and second of all the phantom policy was worth a million dollars. She definitely had a reason to see her husband dead.

"When Marcel and Juliette Madison walked into your agency to get their policy written, how would you judge their demeanor?"

"Well Marcel, the gentleman no longer with us today, was a little intimidated by his wife, but she was a handful," he said nodding at Jewels.

"Can you explain?"

The Truth:

Marcel and Juliette were sitting in his office, going over their insurance policy. At this point they already had five conversations on the phone, and the meeting was just to clear some things up and to get their signatures.

"So this policy is for one hundred thousand dollars," Ansel Gord said to the couple, from the other side of his desk. "And I have included all of the items you requested Now if you can just sign right—"

"That's not going to be enough," Jewels said interrupting him. "Money that is. And that's what we wanted to meet with you personally about. We would like to up the policy for one million dollars. You see we just got married and I can't afford to take care of his funeral expenses, since he has a really hectic lifestyle, in the event something happens to him. I'm going to need a policy that will help me cover our home and everything else."

Ansel was a little taken aback by how Jewels was acting, but he looked at Marcel who seemed under the influence. "Sir, is this what you want?"

"Of course," he said, rubbing his hand over his face, "you heard my wife. Up the joint to a mill."

"Are you high?"

"Fuck no!"

"Can I ask what caused the major turn around?" the agent continued.

"I caused the major turn around," she yelled. "Didn't you hear me? Now do yourself a favor, write up the fucking policy before I go get it from somewhere else."

In The Courtroom:

After the prosecutor got everything he needed to assassinate Jewels' character with a huge grin he said, "No further questions, your honor."

CHAPTER 28

In The Courtroom:

Things were looking terrible for Jewels, due to the latest witness testimonies. But now Adele was ready to pull the trigger, and use her final bullet. After the usual formalities of getting the name and spelling of the witness, Adele welcomed Gina Madison, Marcel's mother to the stand.

Gina's stiff red wig hung over her face, and appeared to highlight the many moles all over her nose. She was sixty years old in the face, even though she just turned fifty the other day. She looked as if she lived a hard life.

"Mrs. Madison, can you tell the court what kind of person your son Marcel Madison was?"

"Very, very, evil," she said in a low voice. When asked to speak a little louder by the judge she leaned forward and said, "Marcel was evil," she looked at Adele, "of the worst kind."

Adele was trying to contain her happy composure, but it was extremely hard. After all, mothers generally side with their children in murder cases whether right or wrong. Gina was already proving to not be the norm, and this could be the breakthrough her case needed.

"And why do you say your son was evil?"

"He was spoiled rotten, and felt entitled to everything. Which is why I believe Juliette when she said he tried to stab her, and she had to defend herself by taking his life. And I say this as his mother."

"I object," the prosecutor yelled. "It is not the witnesses job to tell the court what she believes."

"Objection sustained," the judge said.

"I'm sorry," Gina replied, "I didn't mean to cause any problems." She focused back on Adele. "Like I was saying, my son was very evil, and when he was coming up he tried to kill me once by stabbing me." She pulled the collar of her blouse down, leaned her head to the right and showed a stab wound rolling along the side of her neck. "I woke up just in time to save my own life."

"Mrs. Madison, would you be so kind as to tell the court what happened the night he stabbed you?"

"Sure."

● ● ●

The Truth:

It was Christmas morning and Gina was up all night getting things prepared for her sons. Two bikes sat under the tree with big silver bows on top, a red one that belonged to her son Namon, and a blue one, which belonged to Marcel.

After making sure everything was nice, she called her boys to the Christmas tree. As usual, Namon was very appreciative of his gift, and told his mother how much he loved his new bike. Marcel, on the other hand was not so pleased and acted snotty.

After not having gotten his gift the way he wanted, Marcel threw himself on the couch, and pouted while looking at the bike. "That's the wrong one," he told his mother. "You got the wrong one!" he pointed at it with a stiff finger. "You always do that!"

"Son, it's the same bike." She walked up to him. "I used the picture you left for me on my bed to buy it. You know, the one you clipped out of the newspaper."

"It's the wrong one," he yelled louder. "I wanted the black color. I specifically told you black, but you wouldn't listen. You never listen to me."

She laughed realizing that her fowl up was color related, and not item related. "Oh, son," she giggled. "I'm sorry. I didn't even think to ask about the color. I just grabbed the bike."

"But the one I clipped out was black," he yelled louder. "You weren't paying attention, you never paid attention! That's why daddy left you!"

Gina walked over to her son and sat next to him. "I know you're upset, son, but it's still the same bike. Take it around the block and go enjoy yourself."

With his arms folded over his chest, he stomped toward his bedroom where he stayed all night. But later that evening, while Gina slept in the bed, Marcel climbed over top of her with a butcher knife.

He held it closely to her neck and said, "I should kill you for not getting the one I wanted. You always do that. Always choosing Namon over me. But I won't kill you because I love you." He pricked the flesh of her neck, and licked his lips when he saw her throat opening up and blood oozing out. "But you are taking that bike back, and getting me the right one in the morning. Understand?"

"Yes, Marcel," she cried softly. "Please don't hurt your mother. I love you."

After that incident, and similar ones like it, she put him in a military school to protect herself and Namon, where he stayed until the twelfth grade.

● ● ●

In The Courtroom:

"Do you think he hated you for putting him in that school?"

"I know he did. And he acted up in different ways."

"Do you have any idea on what caused him to be that way? Violent that is?"

"Marcel was picked on a lot at school. His brother too but Marcel never knew how to handle his problems."

"Did something happen to him as a child?"

Her head lowered. "Marcel's father was in his life, in both of my sons' lives, but he was arrested for beating them badly. He would starve the boys while I was at work, and by the time I came home they were already in bed. It wasn't until Marcel was in the hospital, for his father choking him to a point of unconsciousness that I realized something was going on in my home, behind my back. Their father was arrested immediately after that."

After a few more questions, the prosecution cross-examined Gina but her testimony stood the test of time.

Adele called her next witness, and when everyone saw his face, and his gait, they all gasped. The gray designer suit he wore, with the light blue shirt, hung off of his body, better than a Bloomingdale store's mannequin. He seemed regal and more than anything confident. It was as if they were looking directly at Marcel even though there were extreme differences. A pin could be heard dropping, as he stepped into the stand, and was sworn in. This was truly the most interesting part of the case.

"Namon Madison, what relationship are you to Marcel Madison?" Adele asked.

"He's my twin brother."

Jewels sat there, with her jaw on the floor. She had no idea that Marcel had a twin brother. He never mentioned anything about siblings for that matter. Although Namon was similar to his brother, his facial expressions were more relaxed and his eyes were kinder.

"Can you tell us what kind of brother he was?"

He exhaled, looked down and then back at Adele. "Marcel was very cold. He was very angry all the time and for no reason. When he came home from the military school mom put him in"— he looked at his mother and she smiled— "he was nicer, but in a fake way. It was like he was trying to prove to people that he was something he wasn't. Like the school had changed him, and it was the best thing that ever happened. But it was all fake."

"What do you mean?"

"Well he would act like an angel in front of ma," he sighed, "but when she was gone he was always hitting and pushing me. When I would tell him to stop, he would demand that I not be gay. In then when I'd tell him to leave me alone, he would rape me. Put his penis in my anus and make me suck it."

The courtroom gasped again and the judge brought down his gavel, silencing everyone immediately.

"Can you explain how he raped you?"

He swallowed and looked upon the audience. "My brother had been raping me for sometime. He said our father did it to him, but I don't remember things that way. I blocked out a lot of the time back then, because it was all too painful."

"That must have been terrible, how did you manage?"

"It was hard, because I loved my brother. Even though he's gone, I still love him to this day. But he tortured me everyday we lived together, and to tell you the truth, I didn't get a rest from him until Jewels took his life."

"Did you ever report him?"

He sighed. "Yes, plenty of times, but nobody wanted to listen to me," he shrugged. "I guess that's the way things go." He looked at his mother again, and it was obvious he had a lot of pain in his heart. "He broke my leg twice, my right arm once, killed all of my pets and would make fun of me when we were out in front of his friends. He just hated me. So I left, started a life of my own in Arizona, and I hadn't been back, until now."

CHAPTER 29

In The Courtroom:

Howard Murray approached the jury to give his closing remarks. He tried to walk slowly, for affect more than anything else. But it really just showcased his beefy body.

"Ladies and Gentlemen of the jury, I know this is a difficult case, a very hard one. Across the room you see the beautiful Juliette Madison"— he pointed at her— "and you want so desperately to believe her innocence, and to believe she is not capable of anything so gory. But I want to say to you that I do not want you to make your decision, based on a popularity contest, based on who is beautiful, and who is unattractive. But based on justice. I do not want you to place a conviction against anyone who is innocent, so if you think she is innocent, let her go. But"— he wagged his finger from the left to the right of the jury— "lets talk about what it means to be innocent for a moment."

"Marcel Madison was innocent. Yes it is true, that he might not have been the best husband, the best brother, the best son or even the best man, but he is still innocent as it pertains to having a right to live. And even if you call him a cheater or a rapist it does not mean that Juliette, in her rage, had the authority to take his life!" He slammed his fist into the middle of his hand. "She acted as judge, jury and executioner, and for that she must pay!

"Do you hear me good people? She…must…pay, and be held accountable for her actions! So let us be brave, and let us be faithful to our country, and to the laws of our land. If the defendant is entitled to her freedom let her have it, but only make the firm decision to release her, after you have ensured yourselves that she is absolutely not responsible for this heinous crime. The man was murdered in cold blood people, and he deserves justice, and it is up to you to give it to him. Thank you."

When he sat down Adele stood up and approached the jury. Her walk was slow, and methodical and the jury was captivated.

"Juliette Madison is innocent," she said in a low voice. "It's simple and to the point. But why is she innocent?"

She leaned against the jury's stand, directly in front of one of the jurors who had been enamored by her the entire case. From the standpoint, he could see a little of her cleavage, which was her chief aim. "She is innocent because she activated the right that all of us in this country possess, and that is the right to defend ourselves against harm.

"You heard his mother. Gina testified that he stabbed her on the neck, just like he tried to stab Juliette. You heard his brother; he took advantage of him sexually, just like he did Juliette. You heard his many lovers, he lied to them all, just like he did Juliette. Marcel was not a man of honor; he was a man of circumstance.

"If the prosecution asks that we forgive Mr. Madison's many fallacies, we will also ask that you forgive her beauty, since it is obvious that it is being held against her here today. Yes, she is beautiful"— she walked from left to right in front of the jury stand, slowly, and elegantly— "and yes beauty in this country brings with it certain privileges, but none of those things matter here today. What matters is that Marcel Madison intended to take Juliette Madison's life, and she made a decision, in that terrifying moment, to defend herself. To defend her right to live.

"Free her," she said softly. "Let her go home with the hopes of building a family. Allow her the opportunity to start all over, and get her life back on track, for she has been through enough. Please, free Juliette Madison! It's the only fair thing to do. It's the only thing that is right. Thank you."

When she was done the jury deliberated for four hours. And when they returned to the courtroom, everything was on pause. Jewels, and her attorneys stood up, and held onto her sweaty hands.

After the judge regained order in his courtroom he said, "Jury, have you reached a verdict?"

The jury forewoman stepped up and said, "Yes we have your honor."

"How do you find?"

"We the people find Jewels Madison, guilty of second degree murder."

The courtroom erupted in a loud applause, and Juliette, who was so certain she would win, collapsed to the floor.

Adele couldn't believe her ears, because she had never lost a case before now. The judge banged his gavel in an effort to bring his courtroom back in order, but it was useless.

This was the case of the century, and Juliette was going to jail.

CHAPTER 30

8 Years Later

2012

Jewels was laying face up on her bunk, in her jail cell. After years of being incarcerated, things were looking up for her. After all, she would be out of jail in her early thirties, and she had already written her book, which she was sure would be a bestseller. She was just about to catch a nap, when someone was brought into her cell.

Jewels had been in the cell alone for the past three months, and she preferred it like that because her beauty automatically made her despised by the other inmates. This was especially true since the male correctional officers showed her favor. But when she saw whom the C.O. was bringing in she was excited.

Courtney's hair was braided backwards, but it didn't take away from her beauty. Her brown skin glowed, and she looked healthy. Courtney had been arrested years earlier for her loyalty, after refusing to leave Dank's body behind a failed robbery attempt at a dealership. Dank's death was the reason Marcel brought Wade into the gang, so Jewels always remembered the crime.

"Oh my, God," Courtney said hugging Jewels, when the cell was closed and locked. "I can't believe it's you. You are still beautiful."

"Thank you," Jewels said under her breath, while smoothing her ponytail backwards. "You know I try not to be too cute around here, it makes some of these bitches insecure."

"Unfortunately for you, you're doing a bad job."

"Thanks, I think." She sat down on the bottom bunk. "So what brings you in here, Courtney?" she crossed her legs.

She sighed, and leaned against the wall. "Got into a fight at the other prison so I was shipped over."

"So you have been locked up ever since the robbery at the dealership?"

"Yep, but I'll be going home next year, thank God. That's if I don't have to strangle one of these hating ass bitches in here." She looked up at the dirty bunk above her. "Sometimes I wonder if I made a mistake by staying with Dank's body, but I didn't want to see him thrown away like he was trash. And in the back of my mind I thought he would survive, you know I was pregnant with his baby when that shit went down."

"Oh my, God, I didn't know," Jewels said standing up. "What happened to the baby?"

"She's beautiful and home with my mother," she smiled. "Trust me, things are looking up." Jewels walked closer to her. "But anyway, I think it's fucked up with all of the money I helped Marcel make on them streets that he couldn't at least put one dollar on my books."

Jewels grew angry, because she knew that Courtney was aware that she was in jail for his murder. "Girl, stop fucking around."

"What you mean?" Courtney asked honestly. "Marcel's greasy ass didn't hit me one time to ask if I needed anything on my books! He just an old foul ass nigga. And then he got the nerve to be living well in Puerto Rico, while he's taking over his brother's identity. I hate his ass now and can't believe I rode with him for so long."

Jewels flopped down on the bed. "Wait...what do you mean?" her heart was thumping and her head was spinning.

"You didn't know? He over there with some white bitch, and they living it up. It ain't going to last long because he's already low on funds and niggas not fucking with him anymore." Finally she focused on the pain on Jewels' face. "I'm sorry, Jewels, I'm being all insensitive and shit. I know you went to jail for killing him, but I figured you knew he was alive, since everybody else does."

"What are people saying?" her eyebrows rose.

"You really don't know do you?"

"Courtney, I'm really confused. Put me up on what's going on."

Courtney sat next to her. "Jewels, when ya'll got into that fight at the park and you stabbed him he wanted you to pay. He called Gia, and a few other people to help him out of the park, and he was almost near death, so you got his ass good. Anyway she came and got him, and took him to the vet who patches up niggas who are shot and can't go to the hospital. The doctor did what he could, and Gia's bum ass lured Namon to that park on some sex shit and they killed him. Stabbed him in the same areas you stabbed Marcel. As you know the police didn't find the body until the next day so they had time to set things up. After that they burned down ya'lls house so that Marcel's fingerprints would be gone, in the event they found some prints belonging to Namon. Twins share the same DNA but different fingerprints."

"But why would he go through all of this? Just to get at me?"

"No, bitch," she laughed. "The FBI was onto Marcel for that murder massacre at Western Vision Motors, and they were closing in on his ass. Even now they trying to find Namon to question him about his brother, but they can't find him because Namon is dead and Marcel is in Puerto Rico living it up."

Later when Courtney went to lunch, Jewels stayed in her cell. She was laying face up on her bed looking at the bottom of the top bunk. "Well played, Marcel. You actually killed your twin brother, pretended to be him and then showed up in court. It's cool though, you and I are gonna dance again. Believe that."

CHAPTER 31

1 Year Later

2013

Marcel was lying on the floor of the boat making love to Gia. Although he didn't have the funds he was accustomed to, it was much better than being in jail. For the moment he didn't have a care in the world, after he bust his nut into Gia's pussy, he kissed her on the lips. Shit was cool until he got up, and saw Juliette looking down on them with a gun, cocked, aimed and loaded.

Jewels stepped onto the boat and said, "Get over there," she looked at Gia. "Both of you."

Gia quickly ran to the other side of the boat, but Marcel moved slowly. When he tried to reach for his gun a few feet over from him, she fired in the air.

"Nigga, don't make me pop you," she warned. "I'm here for a fucking reason."

He hustled to the other side and stood next to Gia. "Wow, so you found out about me being alive, huh? I just knew I did a good job in court," he laughed, looking her over. Jewels' long hair blew in the wind and she was stunning. "You look good, Jewels."

"I know," she said confidently. "But you on the other hand, are still the greasiest nigga I ever met in my life. I can't believe you tried to pin this crime on me, just so the

FBI wouldn't get a hold of you. And then you killed your brother."

"Fuck my brother," he said.

"From what I hear you already did," she replied.

"You so funny, you don't even know what you talking about."

"You said the shit in court," she yelled. "Remember? That's where I got it from."

"It was my brother and father who raped me," he responded. Pain spread over his face. "For years, and my mother knew about it," he said truthfully. "And instead of getting rid of them, she shipped me off. So when I had a chance to bury Namon and make him pay I did. I wish I could get pops too, but he was upstate."

Jewels didn't know whether or not to believe him, but it didn't matter anyway. Because it didn't take away how she felt about him, or what he put her through.

"It doesn't even matter anymore, because this is payback."

"Even after everything you—"

In an attempt to throw her off, he threw water in her eyes before tackling her to the floor of the boat. The gun slid out of her hand and Gia scooped it up.

"I got it, baby," she smiled aiming at Jewels. "Get up, Marcel."

Marcel laughed hysterically as he hopped to his feet. "I love it! Here you were, thinking you were about to finish what you started and the woman you hate more than anything is holding a gun at you," he said looking down at Jewels.

"I see," Jewels responded calmly, before standing up, walking over to Gia and kissing her on the lips. She removed the gun from her hands without a fight and Marcel's jaw dropped. "But did you see that? Who do you think told me exactly where you were?"

Marcel's eyes widened as he looked at his fake best friend. He was beyond betrayed. "Gia, why? After everything I did for you."

"This is business, Marcel. She has money now, and you are kind of broke these days. It's not personal at all."

"All of those times that I didn't listen to Jewels, when she told me that you were a snake, and now I'm finding out that you really are, when my life depends on it, and it's too late."

"What can I say," she shrugged, "you should've listened to your wife."

"So what you going to do now Jewels?" Marcel asked.

"I'm gonna kill you." She looked back at Gia. "Unhook the boat, baby girl." She obeyed and the boat started moving out to sea from its original docked position. "And we are going to make sure that they are never able to find your body again."

He realized his life was over and sat on the edge of the boat. "Jewels, please don't do this. I mean didn't you ever love me?"

"Of course, but first comes love, and then comes murder right?" she winked.

"But it don't have to be this way."

"Sure it does," Jewels nodded. "Before I kill you though, I feel the need to let you know something. I had plans to murder you anyway and claim self-defense. I was going to make you so angry, that you beat me to a pulp, and then I was going to kill you."

"For what?"

"Because I knew that in order to have a best selling book, I would need a story people were pulled to. I was going to kill you, sit in jail awaiting my trial, and then win my case at by claiming self-defense. But you fucked my plan up when you tried to kill me in the park instead. I didn't win, and ended up having to stay in jail and do my time, but now I'm a millionaire. Thanks, Marcel. You made me famous."

He looked at her and shook his head. "You ratchet ass bitch."

"Blame yourself! You spoiled me, and I knew that a regular job wouldn't afford me the lifestyle I'm accustomed to if I killed you or you left me. But, if I went to jail for killing my husband, and wrote a best selling book based on actual events, that I could write my own ticket."

"And what's Gia's profit in all this?" he asked.

"Five percent of all of the money I get for my book." She sighed. "But the rest is going to go to me and my new husband." She flashed her wedding ring, which he didn't notice at first. When she saw the hurt in Marcel's eyes she laughed. "Oh yes, Marcel, I am officially Mrs. Garrick Lake. Can you believe that he would take me back after all of the shit I put him through?"

"You don't even love his square ass."

"I know, but I'll learn to love him, Marcel."

"I should've squeezed harder on your neck," he replied.

"You sure should have, but you didn't. And now you have to—"

Marcel hopped into the water, before she could finish her statement. Jewels rushed in his direction and fired bullets into the sea. She looked into that water for an hour, waiting for him to pop up, but she didn't see him anywhere.

"Did he get away?" Gia asked looking into the water behind her. "Jewels, do you think he's dead?"

"Yes I do," she turned around and looked at her, aimed and fired into her face. "And you are going to join him." Gia fell off of the boat and into the water.

"Picture me rolling with a snake ass bitch. Never again."

EPILOGUE

Juliette Lake was at her first book event in Atlanta, signing copies of her New York Times Best selling novel, *'First Comes Love, Then Comes Murder'*. Her book was a runaway success, because the world was glued to her story when the case was unfolding in the papers. But to read a fiction book based on real events was just icing to the cake. The line was wrapped around the corner and her loving husband stood by her side.

"I'm so proud of you, baby girl," Garrick said kissing her softly on the lips. "I knew you could do this. You went from a shelter to a penthouse suite."

"Thank you, baby," she looked up at him, after handing a customer her signed book, "but I could not have done any of this without you."

"All I did was hold your hand." He rubbed her back softly. "The rest was all you."

After two hours of continuously signing, she was almost done. She was eager to get back to her five star hotel, grab a meal and spend time with her husband, until she saw a familiar face. It was her ex-husband, Marcel Madison.

Jewels felt lightheaded and her hand shook traumatically. She was certain he was about to raise a gun and shoot her. Instead he lifted a copy of her book in the air, which was riddled with bullet holes.

When he got her attention, he walked away. But she knew in her heart that she would see him again.

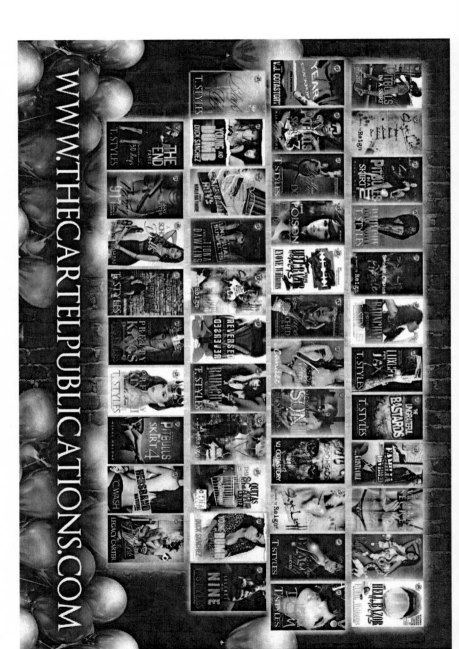

CARTEL PUBLICATIONS

EXTRA RAUNCHY

CHILDREN OF THE CATACOMBS

T. STYLES

NATIONAL BEST SELLING AUTHOR OF *RAUNCHY*

MEAN GIRLS ™

Mean Girls Magazine will offer women the opportunity to reach their full potential in all aspects of their lives, whether it be body, mind or soul. We believe that it's great to embrace your body no matter what shape or size. We believe that the color of your skin doesn't depict how beautiful you are inside or out. We believe it's good to be in tune with your sexuality, and not feel afraid to express yourself in the bedroom. We believe that your dream job may not necessarily involve a nine to five, and we are excited about showing you new and exciting opportunities to launch your career or business. We understand how it feels to be brokenhearted and excluded by those you love, and we support you by accepting you into a community of women just like you.

Mean Girls Magazine is not about being angry, bitter or hateful. It's about being your best, and de-

FOLLOW US:

Facebook: Mean Girls Magazine
Twitter: @meangirlsmag
Instagram: @meangirlsmag

Sign-up for updates on our website
www.meangirlsmagazine.com

The Cartel Collection
Established in January 2008
We're growing stronger by the month!!!
www.thecartelpublications.com

Cartel Publications Order Form
Inmates ONLY get novels for $10.00 per book!

Titles	Fee
Shyt List	$15.00
Shyt List 2	$15.00
Pitbulls In A Skirt	$15.00
Pitbulls In A Skirt 2	$15.00
Pitbulls In A Skirt 3	$15.00
Pitbulls In A Skirt 4	$15.00
Victoria's Secret	$15.00
Poison	$15.00
Poison 2	$15.00
Hell Razor Honeys	$15.00
Hell Razor Honeys 2	$15.00
A Hustler's Son 2	$15.00
Black And Ugly As Ever	$15.00
Year of The Crack Mom	$15.00
The Face That Launched a Thousand Bullets	$15.00
The Unusual Suspects	$15.00
Miss Wayne & The Queens of DC	$15.00
Year of The Crack Mom	$15.00
Familia Divided	$15.00
Shyt List III	$15.00
Shyt List IV	$15.00
Raunchy	$15.00
Raunchy 2	$15.00
Raunchy 3	$15.00
Reversed	$15.00
Quita's Dayscare Center	$15.00
Quita's Dayscare Center 2	$15.00
Shyt List V	$15.00
Deadheads	$15.00
Pretty Kings	$15.00
Drunk & Hot Girls	$15.00
Hersband Material	$15.00
Upscale Kittens	$15.00
Wake & Bake Boys	$15.00
Young & Dumb	$15.00
Tranny 911	$15.00
First Comes Love Then Comes Murder	$15.00

Please add $4.00 per book for shipping and handling.
The Cartel Publications * P.O. Box 486 * Owings Mills * MD * 21117

Name: _____

Address: _____

City/State: _____

Contact # & Email: _____

Please allow 5-7 business days for delivery. The Cartel is not responsible for prison orders rejected.

Personal Checks Are Not Accepted.

CPSIA info
Printed in th
LVOW10s1

451315

9 780989 084512